TABITHA'S REVENGE

Although Tabitha Thomas is only nine years old when her parents die, she vows to travel to London to seek her fortune and gain revenge on Philip Cambridge, the man who wronged her mother. There, Mr Anthony Warren, a wealthy man, decides to turn Tabitha into a beautiful and accomplished lady. But Tabitha never forgets her childhood vow and excitement mounts in this Victorian tale when she effects a return to the Cambridge estate of her youth.

Books by Sara Judge
in the Linford Romance Library:

THE GYPSY'S RETURN
LUCIFER'S HOLD
TUDOR STAR
THE BLOODSTONE RING
THE ORANGE MISTRESS

SARA JUDGE

TABITHA'S REVENGE

Complete and Unabridged

LINFORD
Leicester

First published in Great Britain in 1984 by
Robert Hale Limited
London

First Linford Edition
published 2009
by arrangement with
Robert Hale Limited
London

British Library CIP Data

Judge, Sara.
Tabitha's revenge.- -
(Linford romance library)
1. Orphans- -England- -Cambridgeshire- -
Fiction. 2. Revenge- -Fiction.
3. Cambridgeshire (England)- -Social
conditions- -19th Century- -Fiction.
4. Love stories. 5. Large type books.
I. Title II. Series
823.9′14–dc22

ISBN 978–1–84782–947–4

Published by
F. A. Thorpe (Publishing)
Anstey, Leicestershire

Set by Words & Graphics Ltd.
Anstey, Leicestershire
Printed and bound in Great Britain by
T. J. International Ltd., Padstow, Cornwall

This book is printed on acid-free paper

For My Godchild, Karen Michelle

1

My earliest memories are happy ones. Although my parents were poor, we had a neat little cottage on the Cambridge estate, which was kept in good repair, for my father was head gamekeeper and therefore a man of some standing with the Cambridge family.

I did not know any of them well, for the gamekeeper's daughter was not fit company for Squire's brood; but I knew all the children by sight, seeing the boys frequently as they rode about the estate, and the girls whilst being fitted for dresses by my mother.

Master Philip was the oldest, a tall, dark-haired lad with a thin face and strong nose and chin. He always looked very proud to my childish eyes, and I had seen him close to on but one occasion.

I had been picking blackberries down

by the wood, along the hedgerow which bordered the field from the trees, and the sound of hooves on the turf behind me had made me turn my head.

The younger Cambridge son, Master Mark, was bearing down on me, his horse spattered with mud, and as I stared up at the rider he grinned and swung himself down from the saddle.

'Good-day to you, sweetheart, and what are you called? I don't know you, do I?'

I shook my head. I knew *him*, having often peeped from my window, or gazed from the shelter of bushes, at the dashing Cambridge boys, but he could not know me.

'I am Tabitha Thomas,' I answered shyly, for he was an attractive youth, with a broader face than his brother, and possessing a fairer complexion and very clear, light-blue eyes.

'Old Thomas's daughter?' he said with some surprise. 'I did not know that he had children. Are there more of you lurking in that cottage?'

'Only Mother,' I replied. 'I have no brothers or sisters.'

'Tell me, Tabitha, what do you do with yourself all day long?'

He leaned forward and helped himself to some berries from my basket, staining his mouth with their purple juice and grinning at me like a small naughty boy. I smiled back, for his amusement was infectious.

'Forgive me for prying into your affairs, but I have often wondered how the — er — lower orders spent their time. You don't go to school, do you?'

I shook my head.

'Lucky you! I hate it. Due back next week and I'm dreading the thought. So what do you *do*, Tabitha Thomas?' He gazed at me curiously. 'How do you pass the time? My sisters are forever bemoaning the fact that they must spend so much of the day at their lessons with the governess. But you do not have to worry your head about reading, or writing, or learning French. And you don't ride, or play the piano, I presume?'

I laughed then, and he laughed with me. 'There ain't no room in our cottage for such a thing,' I said.

'Of course not, silly of me. So what do you do with yourself all day long, Miss Thomas?'

Before I could reply we were interrupted by a shout, and another rider came into view.

'Come on, Mark — what keeps you?' he said, as he came nearer. 'Ah, I might have guessed. Now, brother, up on that horse with you and stop molesting the local lasses.' He rode his horse up beside us and stared down at me. 'You don't pick them for looks, do you, my boy?' Master Philip Cambridge looked disdainfully down his nose at me.

'She's all right — the daughter of Thomas, our gamekeeper. Bow to the young lady, Philip. Where are your manners?' chided my companion.

I disliked Philip Cambridge from that day on, for he did not bother to lower his voice and spoke about me as if I were not there.

'Bow? To that brat? You must be out of your mind.' He wrenched at his horse's mouth and the animal reared back on its haunches, making me flinch and step away in fear.

'Don't mind him, he's got no manners,' whispered Master Mark. 'Here, give us a kiss, sweetheart, and I'll be on my way.'

He put an arm around my shoulders and planted a sweet and sticky kiss upon my surprised mouth. Then he released me and leapt into the saddle. 'Farewell, Tabitha Thomas, I'd better not keep His Highness waiting. I'll hear about your doings another time.' With a wave of his hand he began to trot after his brother.

'She's not bad-looking, funny-coloured eyes, though,' I heard him remark as he rode away.

That was my only meeting with the Cambridge boys but the girls I saw more often.

Although Mother could read and write, I was slow in learning my letters and she did not persevere with my lessons. But she always took me with her when she went sewing up at the manor house, and that was how I knew Miss Gwendoline and Miss Verona.

I had difficulty with the alphabet but sewing was a different matter, and Mother often told me that my stitches were as fine and dainty as her own.

I was pleased by her praise but my greatest desire was to possess her looks; Mother was a beautiful woman and the knowledge that I had inherited Father's long nose and mouse-brown hair depressed me at an early age. We had no mirror in our cottage, and I would doubtless never have thought about my appearance had it not been for those sewing visits, and seeing Miss Gwendoline and Miss Verona prinking and cavorting before the long looking-glass. One day when the sisters had been measured by my mother and the resident seamstress and then departed,

I crept forward to view my form in the shiny glass.

I saw a small, skinny, brown-haired child, with thin pigtails on either side of her brown face.

And I possessed yellow eyes.

The shock was so great that I returned quickly to my stool and did not raise my head again until it was time to go home.

No wonder Master Mark had commented on them, and what made matters worse was the fact that the Cambridge sisters were pretty. Master Philip was the only one with black hair and brown eyes; the girls, like their younger brother, were fair-haired, with blue eyes and pink and white complexions. Miss Gwendoline was a little on the plump side, and Miss Verona's hair was straight without a trace of curl, but they were undoubtedly pretty and a pleasure to look at.

Fortunately, Mother and Mrs. Ryan were unaware of my shame, chatting busily about the forthcoming ball, as their fingers stitched and snipped away at their work. But I had seen the truth, and the memory stayed with me for years.

I was christened Tabitha, and it had never occurred to me that when Mother laughingly called me her 'Tabby kitten', and when Father affectionately nick-named me 'Puss', that there was truth in what they said. I looked exactly like a scrawny tabby cat, and felt plain from that day on. Not for me Mother's lovely milky skin and blue eyes, but a brown and yellow combination of ugliness.

Mother chatted merrily on the way home that day about the forthcoming ball which was to celebrate Master Philip's coming-of-age, and how she had caught a glimpse of him the day before, and what a handsome young man he was becoming. Master Philip was known to be his father's favourite, but Mother admitted that she found him arrogant.

'He is too handsome for his own

good, and all the girls are out to catch him, so they say. Mrs. Ryan says that he has sired a good many ... ' She stopped, darting a quick look at me, and then began walking faster. 'Well, never mind that. I think Master Mark is a kinder person, but young girls are always silly about a man's looks.'

She glanced down at me again, then caught hold of my hand.

'What ails you, Tabby? You are so silent. Did you not enjoy our visit today?'

I nodded, clutching at her fingers, holding them tightly for comfort. No one, not even my mother, was ever going to know of my shock and disappointment. I had inherited Father's reticence, as well as most of his features, and feelings, however strongly felt, were locked within my heart, not to be discussed with anyone.

My parents were very happy together. Father could never conceal his love for Mother, and now, with greater awareness, I looked up at her beside me and wondered why she had married him. For besides her beauty, she could also read and write, whereas my father was illiterate. Seeing her up at the big house, moving easily and gracefully through the back rooms, I realised that Mother did not look amiss in such an establishment and seemed ill suited to our little cottage, clean and tidy though it was.

She was also, I think, though it is difficult for a child to judge, many years younger than Father, who always seemed an old man to me. But his love and admiration for her were obvious, and whenever they were in the room together, his eyes would follow her every movement. Indeed, he was really only alive when Mother was present, and if she were out and he and I on our own together, he seldom spoke and would sit quietly, brooding, waiting for the moment when she would open the door and be with him again.

Mother treated us in the same manner, loving to tease and chat, always bubbling over with high spirits and fun. She worked hard, both in our cottage and up at the house, and our lives revolved around her. I was with her always, whether it was cleaning the cottage, cooking or working in our garden, and I also accompanied her on all her sewing trips up to the manor.

Mother wore simple gowns of blue, or brown material, with a starched white apron tied in a bow at the back of her trim waist, and she always wore spotless white caps indoors. Her hair was very dark, very thick and curly, and although it annoyed her, I loved to see the curls escaping from her cap, springing and coiling onto her brow and cheeks.

Mother was rather vain about her caps, I remember, and although we had little money for clothes, she would often sew herself new headgear with remnants of lace and muslin which Mrs. Ryan gave her, up at the house.

Winter and summer alike, she and I wore straw bonnets out of doors, but these were often refurbished with trimmings of ribbon and silk so that we did not feel too dowdy.

Not until we saw the Cambridge sisters, that was. Then Mother would sigh over her needlework and shake her head, and I would see her eyes going longingly towards the piles of silks and velvets and tarlatans, ordered from London, which were to make up the next season's dresses.

I do not remember feeling envious as I stitched away industriously beside my mother and Mrs. Ryan, indeed, I was thankful not to have to wear the petticoats required by the full skirts of those gowns. But Mother, with her sweet face and slender figure, would have looked splendid in fine attire, and I often wished that she could have had lots of money to spend on herself.

But she was never sad or depressed, my mother, and as soon as we had time for ourselves she would be striding out, taking me for walks across the fields, picking wild flowers, or gathering mushrooms in autumn. She loved to sing, and I would join in all the choruses although my voice was never as true as hers. She also made up lovely magical fairy stories for me, which she would tell me last thing at night when I was tucked up in my little bed beneath the rafters.

Looking back now, I realise what a very remarkable woman she was; where did Father meet her? From where did she come? As a child one does not think to ask, and now it is too late.

Being constantly in her company, and loving her as I did, I was quick to notice the change in her that summer of 1839, and her gradual decline in health and humour puzzled and perturbed me. Father was always quiet so I saw no difference in him, but Mother's strange behaviour was alarming.

Now, with the knowledge of a woman, it is clear to me that she experienced a difficult pregnancy, quite apart from the emotional strain. As for Father, he must have been totally stunned by the appalling news, for the child was not his, Mother having been warned by the doctor after my difficult birth, never to have another baby.

But nine years and three months after my birth she produced a second daughter, and Father and I worked together to deliver her.

He would not allow me to run for the doctor.

'No, no, there is no time. She needs us both. Bring hot water quickly,' he commanded, for once brisk in tone and action.

But as the night drew on and Mother's laboured breathing filled the small upstairs room, Father's energy flagged and my heart began to pound with fear. She was ill, deathly ill, and had lost too much blood.

The baby appeared strong and cried lustily as I washed it and wrapped it in a blanket, but Mother was dying, and I shall never forget the sound of my father's sobs as he turned from the bed and sank to his knees, placing his head and arms on the chair, muffling the noise of his grief from his stricken wife.

I crept forward and held on to her limp hand. As long as I held it she could not go away from me.

She opened her eyes, so dark and big in her white face, and she smiled. Then she whispered something, so softly that I could not hear her. Bending forward, I felt her hand slip from my grasp.

'What did you say, Mother? What is it?'

'Philip.' The words floated up to me with her last breath. 'Tell Philip Cambridge.'

Early next morning I went for the doctor, and on our return we found that Father had gone out. He and I had sat in the darkness all night, with the babe occasionally whimpering in the basket, and his tears had ceased and he seemed more in control of himself by dawn. I had not managed a tear; something deep inside me was frozen. All I could think about was Master Philip — rude, handsome, arrogant

Philip Cambridge. And my lovely, laughing mother.

My parents were buried together on a windy afternoon in September. Father had been unable to face life without his adored companion, and his body had been found in the woods on the morning after Mother died, with his gun lying beside him.

There were several offers of help from kindly villagers, but I refused as politely as I could, saying that my aunt in a nearby hamlet would be taking me and the baby in. No one questioned me, or protested too vigorously, for times were hard and life would prove even more difficult with two extra mouths to feed.

That last evening I gathered together my few belongings; a change of underclothes, my Sunday-best gown and the Bible which had been Mother's proudest possession. I had no intention of seeking a home with Aunt May, who was a fierce and domineering spinster. She and Mother had never got on and I had seen little of her during the last few years. In the bitter days and lonely nights after my parents' deaths, I had made up my mind what I was going to do. My decision meant disappearing from this part of the country, leaving my old life, and memories, behind me.

Pleasant memories, that was; thoughts of snug winter evenings round the hearth, listening to Mother reading from the Bible, laughing at the way in which she teased my slow and rather serious father. Those memories were to be pushed far to the back of my mind, they were too painful to bear. And those golden summer days when Mother and I wandered through the meadows, gathering up armfuls of wild flowers, making daisy chains and decorating ourselves with the delicate white flowers. Those I would forget, if it were possible.

What was never to be forgotten was my hatred of the Cambridge family, and particularly of Master Philip Cambridge, for he had robbed me of both a father and a mother, and had destroyed my safe and happy world.

Not one member of the Cambridge family had attended the funeral, although Father had worked on the estate ever since he was a boy, and Mother had been sewing up at the big house for years. I was young, not quite 10 years old, yet the hatred which burned in my thin body was as fierce as any grown woman's could have been.

Apart from inheriting my father's reticence, I also possessed his stubbornness, and on one thing I was now determined. To leave the estate and the county of Hertfordshire behind me, to seek my fortune in London and become, by some miracle, wealthy, clever and beautiful. Then I would return and avenge my parents' deaths.

London was only a name to me then, but I had heard Miss Gwendoline and Miss Verona chattering about it and all the wonderful shops, and the theatres, and the people and the carriages, so the very name had a ring of excitement and magic about it. London was where one could make a fortune, London was where I was going to earn a great deal of money and become a lady. Then I would be able to meet the Cambridges on their own ground and would no longer be looked down upon as a working-class brat.

Early the following morning, as dawn was breaking, I walked over the fields to the drive which wound its long way up to the manor house. My bundle was slung over one shoulder, and in my arms I carried the sleeping infant. I felt no affection for it, nothing save distaste, but I had kept it alive on cow's milk diluted with water. A piece of cloth had been dipped into the liquid, then held to the baby's mouth, and it had sucked with greedy, receptive lips.

That morning I knocked loud and hard upon the front door, taking pleasure in the fact that Bates, the butler, would be rudely aroused from his slumbers. But when he finally appeared he was as perfectly dressed as usual.

Not stopping for words of explanation, I thrust the baby into his reluctant hands, crying, 'Master Philip's bastard — give it to him!'

Then I turned and sped away down the drive, ducking behind some bushes and making for the safety of the woods in case they should send someone after me.

Once I was away and through to the other side of the woods, I walked to the main road and began my journey to London, begging lifts when I could, and walking a good few miles besides. I had a little money, the three gold pieces which Mother had always kept in a pot on the mantel, 'for a rainy day', as she put it. But I would not waste precious money on coach travel and made my way to the city in the back of a wagon, sitting up beside a friendly carter, and on foot.

A clock somewhere was striking the hour of ten in the evening when I was eventually put down in a place called the Strand.

2

There were so many people and horse-drawn vehicles all about me that at first I was dismayed; my country senses unused to such hustle and uproar. I stood back against the window of a shop front and wondered where a place could be found for the night.

As I watched and pondered, a stout, middle-aged lady approached me, very nicely dressed in a warm red shawl and feathered bonnet.

'On your own, dearie?' she queried, gazing at me with little bright eyes in a round face. 'Lost your way, have you? Can I help, perhaps? London is a dreadful noisy and confusing place to a young girl who is new to it.'

'Thank you, ma'am.' I bobbed a curtsey, grateful for this show of kindness. 'I'm newly come from Hertfordshire and am seeking a place to live and somewhere to work.'

'What luck!' She beamed, pulling her shawl more closely across her ample bosom, laying a gloved hand upon my arm. 'I know the very place for you, dearie. You come with me and I'll have you warm and snug this night.'

'Cousin Alice, Cousin Alice — how good to see you again!'

Someone rushed between us, pushing my new friend aside, taking both my hands in hers and laying her cheek against my face in a swift embrace. 'Oh, beg pardon, ma'am, for knocking into you like that, but I was so excited at seeing Alice again I didn't think. Come now.' She turned back to me and held my elbow tightly, steering me through the crowds and away from the older woman, who was calling out angrily behind us. 'Take no notice, come with me quickly, you're lucky I came along when I did.'

'But I don't know you and I'm not your cousin!' I pulled my arm from her grip, indignant at being treated in such a way.

'Shush, don't stop yet, I'll explain later, just follow me and don't look round.'

She dived ahead of me through the crowd, pulling me behind in her wake, and it was some three or four minutes later that she eventually slowed and allowed me to come up beside her.

'What did you do that for?' I rubbed my wrist, which hurt from her fierce grasp.

'I saved you from a fate worse than death, though you're probably too young to know what I mean. But that old witch waits there every evening, looking for unsuspecting country girls. She meets all the coaches which stop in the Strand, and I often see her taking to innocent young girls and then taking them away with her.' She shivered. 'Like a fat spider with a fly. You reminded me of my little sister and suddenly I decided what to do. What's your name?'

'Tabitha Thomas.'

I liked her honest grey eyes and she spoke in a clipped, genteel way, a little like the Cambridge girls. But her face was white and she was very thin and tired-looking.

'Who are you?'

'I am Susan Marsh and you can come home with me tonight. It won't be comfortable or particularly clean,' she shrugged wearily, 'but at least you'll be safe. Whatever are you doing here on your own, Tabitha Thomas? And where is your home?'

'I'm an orphan and I have no home. I've come to make me fortune in London.'

'Ho, ho! That's what they all say. Yet by the look of you you fared better in the country. Those sun-burned cheeks will soon fade and you'll be as thin and white as me before long. Still, I won't nag — come along with me and you can share my supper and my bed.'

Susan led me down a narrow alley and into a small, dark court, which stank abominably. The houses were all crowded in upon each other and numerous children tumbled and fought together in the filth. My companion hurried me across the cobbles to a doorway where the door sagged open upon broken hinges.

'We are up two floors but mind where you tread, some of the boards are rotten. You'd better hold onto me.'

It was very dark in the house and I marvelled that Susan could see her way at all. She led me up two flights of stairs and then stopped at a door on the landing and opened it.

'I'm home, Mother.'

In the flickering light of a candle, I observed a very small room, with a table in the centre and two beds set against the walls. An uncurtained window let in a little light and a woman sat huddled before a meagre fire in the grate. A little girl crouched on the floor beside her. Both turned their heads as we entered, and the child smiled but the woman remained expressionless.

'I've brought some bread and a piece

of cheese, and look, here's a can of milk for our Mary.'

As she spoke my new friend took off her shawl and laid out the provisions which she had folded against her bosom.

'I've brought a friend home with me, you don't mind, Mother? She needed somewhere to sleep and I saved her from Ma Chambers' clutches. If she can find work that'll be more money for us, too. Sit yourself down, Tabitha, and rest.'

I nodded at the woman by the fire, who raised blank eyes for a moment, then continued to gaze at the fire. She was dressed all in black and had a sallow, disagreeable face. She reminded me of a crow. Little Mary ran to her sister, clutching her around the waist, burying her face in her skirts.

'There, Mary, love, aren't you going to say hello? We've got a new friend come to stay with us.'

I smiled at the little girl but she would not look at me and remained clinging to her sister, her face averted.

That was an odd evening, spent in the company of strangers, and though Mrs. Marsh did not utter one word, Susan tried to make up for her silence by chatting to me in a pleasant manner. She was probably glad to have my company, I thought, for her home life was dismal indeed with the silent mother and little shy sister. When Susan heard that I could sew, relief showed on her pale face.

'You must come with me in the morning, Tabitha, and see Mrs. Watson. She is always looking out for girls who are good with their needle, and we have recently lost old Martha who was a most experienced seamstress. The wages are three shillings and sixpence a week, and the conditions are not bad, considering. Also, it is an easy walk from here to Regent Street. If you give Mother two shillings a week for your board, that will leave you with one and sixpence for your very own.'

It seemed a lot of money to me and I

felt that luck was on my side, for I had found a place to live and a place to work within a few hours. I was not sure that I was going to like living in such dismal surroundings, however. We had to go down the stairs and out to the court for our water, and this was from a stand-pipe which was only in use for a few hours each day. And the privies, which served all the inhabitants of the court, were in a terrible state. Holding my breath and treading as carefully as I could in the semi-darkness, I followed Susan back to the house in a very disturbed frame of mind.

At home the air had been fresh and our cottage had been clean and neat. Our food had been plentiful too, whereas all that I had for supper that first night at Paradise Court was a piece of dry bread and some very hard cheese. We drank tea without milk with this frugal repast, for the milk was precious and must be saved for Mary.

At home I had possessed a room and a bed to myself, whereas in London I found that we all slept in the same stale atmosphere and, moreover, Susan's angular body was pressed close to mine all night long.

The following morning, feeling tired and dirty, I accompanied Susan to Regent Street, where I was introduced to Mrs. Watson. Twelve girls were shut at the top of a tall, narrow building, which had a reception room on the ground floor, and a grand apartment on the first floor where dresses were displayed for customers, and there were also fitting-rooms which were lavishly furnished. But the seamstresses were enclosed in an airless room beneath the skylight, and I could imagine how cold it would become in winter, for no heating was allowed for fear of spoiling the beautiful materials with which we worked.

The girls laboured from eight in the morning until ten o'clock at night, and in summer, Susan informed me, and during the Christmas season, they were expected to stay until close to midnight.

They were allowed a half-hour's break at mid-day, and another very short break at five o'clock, and were thus able to rest aching backs and stinging eyes for a short period.

I was by far the youngest and at first Mrs. Watson was dubious about employing me. But after showing her how neat my stitches were, on a piece of cambric which she shoved into my eager hands, the lady put me beside a cross, tired-looking skeleton of a woman and told me to take my orders from Fanny.

Susan was at the other end of the room so we could not converse, but she threw me an encouraging smile before leaving me, and then I settled down beside Fanny and began my work.

I was very tired by the end of that day, for I had never had to sit still for so long before, and realised that the hours Mother had spent helping Mrs. Ryan up at the manor house were luxurious indeed. Here we were expected to work for fourteen hours every day except

Sundays, and I did not think it would be possible to persevere with such drudgery.

'I can't do it,' I said to Susan as we limped home. 'Me eyes ache, and me back aches and . . . '

'What a little moaner you are, to be sure,' Susan said sharply. 'You don't know how fortunate you are in having work. Why, there are many back home in the court who would give anything to be able to bring home a few shillings each week. And we are lucky, really. Old Martha once told me that on the occasion of general mourning for His Majesty William IV, the girls worked from four o'clock on a Thursday morning until half-past ten on Sunday morning. Old Martha said she stood up for much of that time, in order to keep awake, and her legs and feet were so swollen by the end that they overhung her shoes. Now *that* would be something to grumble about!'

'But it is so tiring,' I wailed, not caring about Old Martha, blinking back tears of self-pity and exhaustion. 'Is there not some other work I can do?'

'No, unless you would rather be a scullery maid. Maybe you would feed better, but I don't know about such things and would not know how to get you started in a big house, anyway.'

'What about that kind lady who met me last evening? She said she would look after me.'

Making my fortune in London was harder than I had imagined, and I wanted my mother, and my warm bed at home, and all the freshness and peace of the countryside. The city was too full of dirt and smells and noise, and was overcrowded with people. Thinking of home reminded me of Philip Cambridge, and I clenched my teeth together and felt strength return as hatred surged in my breast. My present misery was due to him, he was the cause of all my loneliness and unhappiness, and I must never allow myself to forget him, or my vow of revenge.

'That's better.' Susan was looking at me with approval. 'Keep your chin up. I could never have allowed you to go off with Ma Chambers, she is a wicked woman and one day you'll understand why. We have also seen better days, Tabitha, but it is no good to keep wailing and whining. One has to just set one's teeth and make the most of one's misfortunes.'

Mr. Marsh had been a clergyman, I learned, and it was after his death that the family had fallen on hard times.

'We never had much money when Father was alive,' Susan informed me, 'but we lived in a small house, all to ourselves, near the church, and our family was united even in poverty. But when he died, we had to leave the house and live elsewhere. I suppose we were lucky to find that room in Paradise Court, but Mother has seen better days, that's why she is so strange, she cannot accept what has happened. And then with both Meg and Tommy going . . . '
She broke off abruptly, biting at her lip.

'Who are they?'

'We don't talk about Tommy. Don't ever mention his name in front of Mother, you hear?'

I nodded vigorously, for her tone was sharp.

'And Meg, well, you might see her. She calls every once in a while to show off her finery, and she sometimes brings Mother small gifts, so I can't stop her coming. But she is wicked, too, Tabitha, and God will punish her one day.'

We trudged down the alley to Paradise Court and my nose rebelled once again as the odours of rotting refuse and the stench from the open sewer hit me full square. Pulling my shawl across my face I ducked my head and followed Susan across the court.

I had wondered how Susan Marsh was so well spoken. Her mother did not utter, and little Mary never spoke above a whisper. There was not a book in the room, nor an ornament or a picture, and the meagreness of the dwelling, which was without curtains or carpet, spoke of abject poverty. Yet Susan talked in a refined way and she could read, and went to church every Sunday. I realised that the family of a parson, poor though they might be, were of a better class than I, and Susan had been reasonably well educated, whilst I could neither read nor write.

I was fortunate in meeting such a one as Susan Marsh, for she was a good girl, caring for her mother and small sister, and also caring about what happened to me. The other girls at Mrs. Watson's were a selfish, ignorant lot and they only talked about themselves and their men friends. Much of what they said was beyond my understanding, but Susan would often tell me that their behaviour and speech were quite abominable and she hoped that I would not learn bad habits from them.

One of the first things I did after starting work was to sew myself a small, draw-string bag. In this I intended keeping my savings; it was to remind me always of my vow, and of my future.

One day I would return to Hertford-shire as a lady; one day I would avenge my parents' deaths.

But first I had to have money, a great deal of money. Unfortunately, saving was difficult, for Mrs. Watson refused to pay me three shillings and sixpence because I was too young. All I received from her was three shillings a week, and with two of those precious pieces given to Mrs. Marsh every Friday, I was left with twelve pence. But the twelve pennies were not put away, for if we broke a needle we had to pay for its replacement; if Mrs. Watson decided that I had been too lavish with my thread, the cost of that, too, was taken from my wages. And buttons, in my cold fingers, had the habit of slipping out of my grasp and rolling under benches and then embedding them-selves between the cracks in the floor-boards, out of reach. These, too, had to be paid for. Sometimes I was lucky to have three pennies for myself at the end of the week.

It was then that I began listening to the other girls, realizing that they, too, found it hard to make ends meet, but most of them had found the solution to their needs. They had gentlemen friends who met them after work, and took them out on Sundays.

'Mr. Jenks give me these last night.' Pretty, black-haired Polly jerked her head over her sewing, making the gold drops in her ears tremble and catch the light. 'So considerate and generous a gentleman, 'e is, an' there's more to come, 'e says, so long as I'm nice to 'im.' And she winked a bold eye, making the other girls laugh.

All except Susan. She flashed a quick look at me and then bent over her work, frowning as she did so.

'Have you a gentleman friend?' I whispered to Fanny, wondering why Susan was so disapproving. Friends who had money were surely a good idea when we earned so little and needed so much. And I should have dearly liked a pair of gold ear-rings.

'They only goes for the young and dizzy ones,' snorted Fanny, straining tired eyes over the lace in her hands. 'Though 'ow they finds time for such goings on beats me. Mind you, I've 'ad me share of compliments and presents, when I were young, like. But it ain't no use me trying for a man now, fair wore out I am by the time I leaves 'ere. But you, Tabs,' she smiled, showing blackened, broken teeth for a moment, 'you've your life afore you, an' if you're clever, like, and don't listen over-much to that prim and proper friend there, you'll get by. Be quite a looker, I reckon, when you're growed up.'

I plied my needle thoughtfully. Susan was kind and I was beholden to her for many things, but I was not saving money and that was the all important thing in life. With money anything was possible, without it I would be doomed to a life in this dreary room, growing to look more like Fanny with every passing year

'An' I gotta new red petticoat for best,' cried out Marjie, who sat next to Polly. There was great rivalry between them although they were supposed to be friends. 'My Mr. Williams is taking me to Brighton on Sunday and I may not come back!'

This remark was followed by shrieks and yells and some comments which I did not understand, then Mrs. Watson threw open the door and stood in the doorway, swelling with wrath.

'If you girls think you are here for a gossip and a chat, you can leave this minute — at once — do you hear?'

There was silence as we bent over our work, needles flying, in and out, in and out.

'I have a customer downstairs and the row overhead is quite appalling. One more sound from any one of you and you can all go. I can get cheaper girls than you and replacements could be found in ten minutes. So that's a final warning. Fanny, you're supposed to be in charge here, what's wrong with you? Too old? Or have you a pain in your gut?'

'Beg pardon, ma'am, just 'igh spirits, ma'am. It'll not 'appen agin.'

'I should hope not, indeed.' Mrs. Watson closed the door behind her with awful gentleness and then we heard the stairs tremble as she made her descent to the lower floor.

Poor Fanny. She was shaking beside me and I saw a tear roll down her face and drop onto her sewing.

'Drat!' she whispered, wiping her nose with the back of her hand. 'She wants me out, I know it. Too old for the job, she says. But if I leaves 'ere I'll never git another job. If it weren't for this wedding coming up and all the trousseau needed in a rush, she'd 'ave me out of 'ere tomorrow.'

3

One day the following summer I saw Meg for the first time. It was a Sunday so I had not gone to work and was sitting with Mary, waiting for Susan to come home from church.

We had had several weeks of fine weather that year, and although the heat increased the stench which arose from the court, it was cooler to sit outside than in the humid atmosphere of our dank little room. Mrs. Marsh would never allow the window to be opened, so the air was foul and very warm.

Doubtless I was becoming used to the city smells, for I quite enjoyed sitting out on the step, watching all the comings and goings at Paradise Court.

Suddenly Mary let out a small excited sound at my side and, looking down, I saw that she was smiling, gazing ahead of her at the crowd of people who thronged the court. I turned my head, wondering what had attracted her attention, and saw a vision in powder blue, with frothing petticoats and the prettiest straw hat, with pale blue ribbons floating from it, picking her way delicately over the cobbles towards us.

Some of the women stopped talking, glancing over their shoulders at the newcomer, and one of them spat almost at her feet. Two men nearby nudged each other and grinned, but a third stepped forward with a bow and offered his arm to the lady. She took it with the sweetest smile and he led her toward us.

Mary stood up and ran forward.

'Mary, love, mind your hands on my gown, are your fingers clean?' Her voice was husky and the laughter in it softened the sharpness of her words. She thanked the man warmly and then glanced about her. 'Gracious me, this place gets worse each time I visit. How can anyone bear to live amongst such filth?' She looked up then and saw me on the doorstep. 'Beg pardon, may I pass through?'

Mary tugged at her hand and pointed with her other. 'Tabitha,' she whispered, 'our friend.'

'Who?' The lady in blue stared at me and I rose quickly to my feet, wondering if I should curtesy. 'Who are you?'

'Tabitha Thomas, ma'am, and I live with the Marshes upstairs.'

She frowned. 'I did not know that they had a guest. Dear me, where do they keep you, Tabitha? In the cupboard?' She let out a small spurt of laughter and then held out her hand to me. 'How de do, I'm sure. I'm Margaret Marsh, Meg to my friends, I expect Susan has told you about me. She never misses a chance to preach.'

Her hand was soft to my touch and she smelt of flowers, reminding me suddenly of the countryside. For one dreadful moment Mother came most vividly to mind and I thought I was going to cry. There had been no beauty or freshness or cleanliness in my life for many a long month.

'Now, Tabitha,' said Meg briskly, gathering up her skirts, 'won't you come up with me to see Mother? I find it so hard to converse with her and don't suppose dear devout Susan is back from church yet, is she?'

I shook my head, swallowing back my tears, longing to be a friend of this exquisite creature. She was like a princess and exactly the sort of person I longed to be. Meg Marsh was small-boned and delicate-looking, with a very white skin and golden hair which hung in ringlets beneath her hat.

'I've brought a few goodies with me,' went on my new companion, and Mary gave a little skip as she pressed close to her sister. 'Don't shove me, Mary, dear, do please go on ahead. I cannot allow this dress to become soiled, it was fresh on today.'

Wondering why she bothered to wear such finery to Paradise Court, I led the way upstairs with Mary following, and Meg bringing up the rear, moving slowly and carefully up the dirty stairs.

Mrs. Marsh did not show any pleasure at the sight of her daughter, but then she never showed emotion. Fortunately, Meg did not seem to mind and chatted away, placing a small packet in her mother's hands, giving Mary another and putting a third beribboned package on the wooden table top. I noticed how white and smooth her hands were. She was a real lady and one could see that hard work and grime did not have a place in her world.

'That's for Susan,' she said, 'though she'll no doubt give it back to me. I'm sorry I have nothing for you, Tabitha, but I did not know that you were here.' She paused. 'I know what you can have!' Her voice lifted and she spun towards me, putting her hands to her breast. 'Here, the very thing, it's only a little trinket but it's pretty and you shall have something from me.' Deftly she

45

unfastened the brooch and held it out to me. There was a blue stone in the middle surrounded by pearls.

'Oh, no, I cannot!'

'Of course you can.' Meg swooped upon me, catching hold of the grubby collar of my Sunday best. It was a gown which Mother had made from leftovers of a dress belonging to Miss Verona; it was my favourite shade of green, with lace at the neck and cuffs. Once I had been proud to possess the garment, but now it was stained and dirty although I only wore it once a week, and I was ashamed of my appearance in front of this beautiful lady.

'Of course it don't go with that colour,' said Meg, stepping back and observing me with narrowed eyes, 'but it's a pretty piece and one day you'll have another, Tabitha Thomas, and we'll make sure it matches your green gown.'

She bent forward, looking at me closely. 'A pity about your eyes — what an odd colour, to be sure. But they are different, and nicely set. One day, Tabitha, when you are older, you could make something of yourself, I've no doubt. If you're ever in need of advice I'll be glad to help you. A girl only has her face and figure to commend her, so she must make the most of those two precious possessions.'

Mrs. Marsh sat holding her present unopened on her knee, but Mary tugged at the wrapping on hers, squeaking with delight as she unfolded a scarlet kerchief.

Suddenly a voice rang out above our merriment.

'I'll thank you to leave us alone, Meg Marsh, and not come spreading your poison here!'

Susan had come up the stairs without our hearing her and now stood, her pale face flushed with anger, her hands clenched at her sides, in the doorway. She looked as shabby and dirty as I, and I could understand her anger. It was, no doubt, due to resentment and envy. We were poor and it showed.

'I suppose you hoped to get away before seeing me,' Susan went on, turning to close the door behind her. Then she strode forward into the room, confronting her sister. 'I heard what you were saying to Tabitha, you wicked girl, and I'll tell you right now that she'll not be coming to you to learn your vile ways. I didn't save her from Ma Chambers' clutches in order to see her grabbed by the likes of you!' She swept the remaining, unopened package off the table with a blow from her right hand. 'And don't come tempting me, either, with your ill-gotten gains.'

'Dearie me.' Meg smoothed down her skirts and winked at me, who was standing ill at ease in the background, hoping not to be noticed. 'How can you stand such a temper, Tabitha? Your church service has done nothing to sweeten your disposition, dear sister, nor taught you to be kind to sinners. What a hypocrite you are, to be sure.'

Susan's face went redder than ever

and she turned with a muffled exclamation towards her mother. 'I'll be getting you a sup of tea, Mother, you must be parched in this heat.'

She removed her bonnet, a sad affair compared to her sister's elegant creation, and I went to place the crockery on the table, glad of something to do. We only possessed three mugs, for Susan and I shared ours, and I wondered if Meg would be wanting something to drink, then one of us would have to go without. But Meg was already moving towards the door. Little Mary ran to her and caught at her hand, covering it with kisses, the gay scarf wrapped around her thin neck.

'That will do, Mary, leave Meg alone, she must not keep her coachman waiting,' Susan remarked in a tight voice. 'I saw him all bored and ridiculous in his white stockings and fine uniform out in the street. I wonder what he thinks of you in his heart.'

'Servants are not paid to think,' Meg retorted, with a toss of her head.

'Goodbye, Tabitha.' She flashed me a quick smile before opening the door. 'Don't forget what I said — your face will have to make your fortune, my dear, nothing else will help you to survive in this dreary old world.'

'Bah!' Susan sped across the room and slammed the door behind our visitor, making large flakes of plaster fall from the ceiling onto the bare floor boards. 'How can you allow her to come here, Mother? Poor Father would turn in his grave if he could see his eldest daughter now.'

Mrs. Marsh did not answer but remained staring into space. The small packet which Meg had given her still lying in her motionless hands.

What a strange family.

Later, when Susan had calmed herself and we had gone to bed, I dared to ask a few questions. Susan would not say much, but I learned that Meg lived with a gentleman in a part of London called St. John's Wood, with her own furniture and servants to look after her, and she was a whore. Susan would tell me nothing more save that Meg was a very bad woman and would surely go to Hell.

I wondered if my mother had been a whore, for she had not been married to Philip Cambridge, yet she had produced his child. It was all very muddling and sad and I could not bear to think that Mother was not in Heaven, nor did I consider her a bad woman. She had been loving and laughing and gentle, it was Philip Cambridge who was the wicked person, destroying both my parents and ruining my life. Yet he remained alive. One day, when I was older, I would understand but for the moment I was puzzled and very homesick. Screwing myself up into a ball with my face away from Susan, I tried to control my tears, vowing all over again that somehow I would become a wealthy and beautiful lady, looking just like Meg Marsh, and would make Philip Cambridge suffer for all the misery he had caused.

During the next three years I worked long and hard for Mrs. Watson, miraculously preserving my health, whilst watching Susan Marsh become thinner and more irritable with every month. She took too much upon herself, labouring for her little sister and silent mother. I did what I could to help and tried to remain cheerful, but there was never enough food or money to go round, and Meg visited seldom, and then only brought silly trifles when a few shillings would have made all the difference to our lives.

The worst problem was water, for the stand-pipe in the middle of the court was only in use for a few hours each day when Susan and I were away from home. Little Mary was supposed to carry her bucket and take her place in the queue, but she was so small that most often she was pushed to one side, or her pail was knocked and the precious contents spilt. In winter the pipe froze and sometimes we would be days without any water at all.

Often I would think longingly of the well back home in our garden, and remember the sweetness of that water and the limitless supply. In London we could never wash ourselves, for that would be sheer waste. All we could do was use it for cooking and drinking, with a small amount saved for a Saturday evening when we would wash the few garments we possessed.

Soon after I arrived at Paradise Court, I realised that Mrs. Marsh drowned her sorrows in gin, and Mary was often running to the gin shop round the corner in the Strand for her mother's liquid comfort. I grew to despise the woman, for although she never spoke she was able-bodied and was surely capable of going out and finding work. But she preferred to sit in misery and allow both daughters to suffer whilst she drank and grieved.

Susan and I had no such solace; Susan frowned upon the consumption of liquor and I did not care for the taste. Maybe the girl found comfort in her church, but for me it was the thought of money which consoled me slightly, and I saved every possible penny and farthing in my calico bag.

By the time I was 13 years old the magical sum of four pounds had been saved. Mother's gold pieces had not lasted long, for new clothes and shoes had been needed as I grew in stature, but my savings were special, earned by my own hands, and whenever gloom settled upon me I would shake out the money on to the floor and count the coins one by one, gloating over them and the hope that they gave me.

Then cholera swept through the court, coming so quickly and taking its deathly toll so rapidly that at first we could scarcely believe what was happening to us. I believe thousands died all over London, but I was only aware of the deaths in Paradise Court, and Susan Marsh was one such victim.

She did not die of the cholera, but would go out tired as she was after work, and tend the sick and dying. This extra work proved too much for her frail body and she died, so the harassed doctor told me briefly, of exhaustion.

It was at this time that I first discovered what had happened to Tommy Marsh, whose name was never mentioned. When the clergyman, Mr. Marsh, had died, his family had been left destitute and had spent some months after his death in St. Pancras workhouse. Then Susan had found herself work with Mrs. Watson, and the room in Paradise Court, and had rescued her mother and little sister from their miserable existence in the workhouse. But she had been too late to save Tommy, who had been apprenticed from the Parish, with two hundred other children, to a far-off cotton mill in Lancashire. Meg, I ascertained, had very soon found her gentleman friend and gone off to live a life of luxury and sin, but the Marsh family had never seen Tommy again.

Now, with Susan's death, Mrs. Marsh suddenly awakened from her lifeless state and declared that her daughter was not to be buried until all the family were present. And it took over a week for the news to reach Tommy, and for him to make the long journey south to London. A week, whilst Susan's poor body lay upon the bed and I had to choose between placing myself beside Mrs. Marsh and Mary, or else lying my body upon the hard and draughty floorboards.

There was also the problem of money. Although I missed Susan both at home and at work, I cannot admit to having loved her, and with her corpse before me for every minute of the time that I was in Paradise Court, I began to hate her wretched lifeless form. The atmosphere in that small room had been vile enough before, but my senses had become used to it. Now, the stench became intolerable and I could neither eat nor sleep.

'She must go!' I shouted at Mrs. Marsh. 'It is not right to keep her body in here with us.'

But Mrs. Marsh, finding her voice at last, was adamant.

'Susan remains until all the family are gathered together, and besides, we must be sure that she is dead. I watch her all day long and will know if she stirs. We could not condemn her living to the grave, now could we?' And she fixed me with her dark, brooding eyes.

I shivered and little Mary crept closer to me. She had not spoken a word since her sister's death, and I wondered dismally if she would be the next to go.

'We also need four pounds to bury my daughter. Susan had nothing put by.'

I looked into the woman's haunted face and felt anger and dislike surge within my bosom. She knew that I had money; there were no secrets in that small room, and although Mrs. Marsh appeared listless and devoid of interest, how often had she seen me counting out my pence, gaining comfort from the shiny round pieces? Oh, yes, she knew about my precious savings for which I had laboured long and hard these past years.

'Ask Meg,' I said sharply. 'She is family and I am not.'

'Meg has given enough — ever generous, my eldest daughter. But you,' her lip quivered, 'you were brought here, fed and sheltered by Susan. She found you work and cared for you. The least you can do to show gratitude is to pay for her funeral.'

Meg must help me. I would offer to pay half, but not all my savings. I could not bear to see them vanish completely. It also occurred to me that now, with Susan gone, I would become the sole wage-earner and would have to keep three people on my three shillings a week. Mrs. Watson still did not pay me the extra sixpence, although I was old enough now and a fully experienced seamstress. Mrs. Marsh could be abandoned without regret, but I could not desert Mary, who clung to me as she had once clung to Susan. And she was too weak and poorly to find work for herself, I could not leave her alone with her useless mother.

Meg would have to be confronted; with her fine home and secure position, she could take over her family's responsibility leaving me free to branch out on my own. I would need her advice, too, as to how to find a gentleman friend. Now that Susan was gone I need not fear her frowns or scolding, and would seek the protection of a man who would look after me. That would be the answer to all my problems.

Tommy arrived the evening before the funeral, a pale, pitifully thin lad of some eleven years. His foot had been caught in machinery two years before so that he walked with a slow dragging limp.

That first night he was too tired to talk, and after swallowing a morsel of bread he curled up beside me on the floor and slept unmoving, all night through.

His mother had tried to take him into

her arms, making strange crooning noises in her throat, but the boy had pulled away, looking bewildered and uncomfortable by this display of affection.

Next morning the undertaker arrived and Susan's remains were placed in a plain wood coffin. Meg also arrived, looking sad and beautiful in black velvet, with a becoming bonnet which had black plumes on it, and a veil which did not conceal the loveliness of her features. She would not enter the room but stayed out on the landing, holding a tiny lace handkerchief to her nose.

'Dear heavens, Tabitha, have you all gone mad?' she exclaimed, as we trooped out to join her. 'How could you live in there all this time with that — that . . . ' she broke off, words failing her.

'One gets used to anything,' I answered dully, 'taking Mary by the hand,' and your mother wished it so. We all know for certain now that Susan is dead. Please, Meg, do not go before talking to me. I need your advice.'

She nodded, then, catching sight of Tommy, moved to his side as I led Mary down the stairs behind Mrs. Marsh.

I paid for Susan's burial, as I knew I must, and my little calico bag sagged empty in my hands. Four years of hard labour were spent on a cheap wooden box and a hole in the ground. But there was no one else to pay and even though I begrudged the money, I could not allow my friend to go to a pauper's grave.

Meg had not been helpful.

'I'm sorry, dear Tabitha, but John gives me no money. He pays for my clothes, and sees to all the bills, of course, but no coins pass from his hands to mine.' She gave a little toss of her head. 'Too common!'

She was equally unhelpful about her family and its future. 'I could not possibly have them live with me, can't you understand that? John has made me what I am and is rightly proud of me. But he has often said that although I come from the gutter I must never, by word or deed, give away my past. Can you imagine what his friends would say if they knew that I had spent some time in the workhouse!' She gave a delicate shudder. 'It is very good of him to allow me to visit Paradise Court from time to time, but that is only because I don't stay long and am accompanied by a trusted servant who can keep his mouth shut. No, dearest Tabitha, much as I grieve for you, I could never have Mother or Mary to stay.'

'Then perhaps you could tell me how to find a gentleman friend,' I said, 'for it is obvious that my wages must now support three people and 'tis not enough.'

'If you want a gentleman of quality you must smarten yourself up, Tabitha.' Meg surveyed me critically, lifting her veil to see better. 'I'll bring some of my old gowns and petticoats next time I come, and for goodness' sake wash yourself. Any girl can get a man down the Haymarket, but you'll need a clean face and tidy hair if you wish to attract the attentions of the gentry.'

Mrs. Marsh caught up with us then and Mary ran forward to take my hand, so I did not get the chance to speak to Meg again on the subject. Her carriage was waiting for her in the Strand on our return, and she did not come back with us to Paradise Court.

Tommy spent that last night with us before his journey back to Lancashire, but he was very quiet and I wondered why his sister's death should have so affected him. He had not seen Susan, or his family, for six years, and it would be a further ten before his apprenticeship ended and he could leave the mill.

'Are you happy there?' I asked, as we made ready to sleep. 'Do they work you hard?'

'We begin work at six in the morning and stop at 'alf seven at night, an' I 'ates it there!' He burrowed down beneath the blanket on the floor, hiding his face from me.

'I have to work hard, too, Tommy, but it is not so bad if you can save. Do they pay you wages during your apprenticeship?'

'One an' sixpence a week.'

'That's not much.' I sat beside him, hugging my knees. We were still on the floor, I could not face the bed yet with memories of its recent occupant. 'Dearie me, when will you be free to leave?'

'When I'm 21.'

Suddenly I heard an odd snuffling sound and I looked down at him cautiously. If he were crying he would not want me to know. 'Tell you what, Tommy, I've bin thinking a lot about our future and I've got some good ideas. Now you stay on at that mill and be a good boy and work hard, and then by the time you come back to London I'll be a real lady and have lots of money and you can come and stay with me. How does that sound?'

'Can't wait that long — not going

back — can't bear it, Tabs.' He lifted himself up on to one elbow, pushing back the blanket, his white face wet with tears. 'They straps us, Tabs, when we fall asleep an' holds us in a cistern full of water, 'ead down, when we gets drowsy. An' you gotta keep going 'n' all those machines keep roarin' and the wheels go round and round, clanking and banging, an' it's hot and smelly an' I 'ates it!'

He bunched his fist and beat it before him on the floor. 'We don't get enough to eat and we're always tired an' my best pal died last month — knocked down, 'e were, by the overlooker, and 'e fell into the machines an' I *saw* it, Tabs.' He broke off, lowering his head onto his hands.

'Tommy,' I said, laying my hand gently on his rough hair, 'Tommy, you got to be brave 'cos there's no way out. But think of the *future*, Tommy, and I'll work real hard down here for you — for us all — and we'll come through in the end, you see if we don't.'

4

The Sunday after Tommy went back to the mill, as he had to, I spent refurbishing Susan's best gown. She had been taller than I but I put up the hem and sewed some lace around the collar. This last had been stolen from Mrs. Watson's. It was only a remnant and a poor piece at that, but there were strict rules about taking oddments home with us, and if I had been caught my punishment would have been severe. But I was desperate; desperate for a new dress, intent on making a good impression, in dire need of money. And I could not wait for Meg's next visit. Mrs. Marsh needed her daily tots of gin, and little Mary looked as if she would soon follow her sister to the grave. We all needed food and warmth, and the rent had to be paid. So I took Susan's faded blue velvet, pinned Meg's brooch beneath the lace collar and washed my hair for the first time in weeks.

Fleetingly, I wondered if it would be possible to go through with my plan. In the four years that I had been with Mrs. Watson I had learned a great deal about life, and in summer Paradise Court was filled with couples who left the stuffy atmosphere of those narrow dwellings and copulated openly in doorways and on the dirty cobbled courtyard. Susan had tried her best to shield me from the coarser side of life, but I had seen enough to know what I had to do, to realise what it was that my mother had done with Philip Cambridge.

I did not want a baby, but Meg had not produced an infant in all the time that she had been with her gentleman, and both Polly and Marjie were carrying on with their gentlemen but had remained childless, so perhaps I would be lucky, too.

Thus I prepared myself for the fate

from which Susan had tried so hard to save me.

I left Mrs. Marsh sitting before the empty grate, her eyes glazed and her breath heavy with gin fumes; Mary slept and Tommy had gone. I put on my bonnet and my shawl and ventured forth to the Strand. There were still a great many people about at this hour of the night and I was pushed and jostled by the crowd as I made my way towards the Haymarket.

The theatres and music halls were ending their entertainment, and amongst the throng I noticed some well-dressed and elegant gentlemen who I hoped might notice me. But as I paused, moving back against the building beside me to take stock of the situation, I saw that all these gentlemen were accompanied by beautifully attired ladies; they would not do at all. They climbed into waiting carriages and were driven swiftly away.

As I watched, I saw other ladies, with brightly painted faces, none too well dressed, who stopped before single gentlemen and lifted their skirts a few inches above their ankles. It was a brazen way to act, but it was suddenly clear to me that they were street women, and this was the manner in which they attracted the attention of prospective customers.

Taking a deep breath I moved a few steps forward, searching the oncoming people for a friendly face.

Then I saw him, so tall that he was head and shoulders above the other men. He was dressed in evening clothes and his shirt front was very white, his top hat very shiny. He looked clean and smart and not unkind. And he was alone.

I stepped forward into his path and lifted my skirts.

'Please, sir.' I could think of nothing else to say.

'What the devil!' He frowned down at me in the gaslight. 'What are you doing here at this hour of the night?'

'I want you to take me home with

you — I need money so badly, sir. And I washed me hair last night,' I added quickly.

'How old are you, for heaven's sake?'

'Fourteen, well, nearly. An' I never bin with a gentleman before but I'm willing to learn and I'll do me best for you and you won't be disappointed.'

'Where are your parents and what is your name?' He spoke very quietly.

'I'm an orphan and me name's Tabitha Thomas.'

'There are other ways of earning a living, Tabitha Thomas. Why don't you get yourself an honest job, you look strong and healthy enough to me.'

'I have a job, sir, but it don't bring in enough — I need much more.'

'How mercenary!'

I liked the sound of that word. 'Yes, sir.' I smiled. 'And do please take me with you, you'll not regret it.'

'I have no intention of taking you anywhere and would advise you to get back wherever it is you live and go to sleep, or you'll not wake up in the

70

morning and will lose the work you already have. Great heavens, girl, you're earning a wage and should be satisfied. Greed is not a quality I admire.' He made to push past me. 'Get on home with you before you are arrested.'

'But we can't live on three shillings a week,' I wailed, catching at his sleeve. 'The rent's two shillings and we've got to eat, and I want to save something — me money's all gone. Oh, won't you give me a chance, sir?'

'What did you say?' He spun round so sharply that I fell against him, knocking my bonnet sideways over my face.

'I said give me a chance,' I muttered, resettling my bonnet upon my head.

'Before that — how much do you earn?'

'Three shillings, and it's not enough.' I tilted my chin and stared angrily up at him. 'All me savings are gone on account of Susan's burial, and I've gotta start again, and I don't know how I'm ever . . . '

'Perhaps you do need help, Tabitha Thomas,' said the gentleman. 'Do you mean to tell me that you collect three shillings after a week's labour? What do you do, girl? And how many of you have to live on that pittance?'

'Mrs. Marsh and little Mary and me,' I answered, 'an' there's food and Mrs. Marsh's gin to get, an' milk for Mary, and the rent to pay, an' candles and coal and . . . '

'All right, all right,' he lifted his hand, 'that's enough. Can you read, Tabitha?'

'No, sir.' What did he want to know that for?

The gentleman sighed, the he placed his hands behind his back and leaned forward.

'Then how is your memory, girl? Can you remember my address if I tell it to you?'

Hope lit up within me and I smiled. 'Me memory's ever so good, sir, you tell me where you live an' I'll come whenever you want.'

'Then come to number twelve, St.

James's Square, at eleven o'clock tomorrow morning. And my name is Anthony Warren.'

I nodded. 'I'll not forget, sir. But,' I hesitated, 'it'll mean losing me job. Mrs. Watson don't keep us if we have time off. Even if we're sick she expects us to go else she dismisses us.'

'You can forget about that wretched job, Tabitha. Come along and see me and we'll sort something out.'

'Oh, thank you, sir.' I bobbed a curtsey, my heart thudding with joy. Perhaps I'd get a little house in St. John's Wood. And I'd make sure that Mrs. Marsh and Mary were looked after, too. If he wouldn't let them come to stay, if he were too particular, like Meg's John, then I'd take them money once a week. They would get their rent and their food, on that I was deter-mined.

The next morning I found my way to St. James's Square. Number twelve was a very tall building and the railings outside were black and shiny, like my gentleman's top hat. The front steps were polished red and the front door was white with a gold knocker on it. It was set so high that I could hardly reach it, and my rat-tat-tat seemed not so loud as the beating of my heart. But somebody heard, for the door opened almost at once and a most superior butler, who bore a remarkable resemblance to Mr. Bates who had served the Cambridge family, looked down at me.

'Wait here, if you please,' he said, looking and sounding very displeased about something. Then he left me in a high-ceilinged dark hall and marched up the stairs to a floor above.

I fingered my skirts, smoothing the worn material and wishing that there had been something better to wear than Susan's blue velvet. But my working dress would not have done for such an appointment, and my Sunday best was shabbier than Susan's.

I clasped my hands before me to restrain their uneasy movements, and gazed at the oil paintings on the walls, and at the door beside the stairs which was shut, and at the thick red carpet which covered the floor in the hall and carried on up the stairs to where a curve hid any further view.

Where was the gentleman's bedroom? Swallowing down my fear I waited.

Some minutes later the butler reappeared round the bend in the stairs and stood on the little landing looking down at me.

'Follow me, miss. Mr. Warren is waiting.'

I climbed the stairs behind him, round the curve and up another flight to the first floor. Here were two doors to my right and left, and the butler led me to the one on the right.

'The young person is here, sir,' he announced stiffly, then he bowed and withdrew, closing the door behind him.

It was not a bedchamber but a large sitting-room, filled with a great deal of furniture, with lovely green curtains by the window, and gold striped wallpaper.

My gentleman was standing in the middle of the room on a thick and multi-coloured carpet.

'Good-morning, Tabitha Thomas, I see that you have found me all right. Please be seated and remove that monstrous bonnet.'

He indicated the sofa with his hand and I sank onto the green silk-covered sofa and took off my poor little headgear.

'It's the only one I have,' I said, looking at it in my hands, 'some flowers would look nice, or perhaps a feather, but I don't have . . . '

'I know, I know, you don't have the money,' he remarked, moving forward to sit in a chair opposite me.

He was wearing brown checked trousers and an elaborate waistcoat of green and yellow. Around his neck was a canary-coloured silk cravat, and his side whiskers were thick and dark brown, like his hair. He was a very handsome gentleman.

'Well, now, Tabitha,' he went on, 'I

have been thinking about you and have come to a decision. I have a proposition to make to you . . . '

'I am quite willing, sir, and very grateful. But I must be back by ten this evening, else Mary will worry.'

'Do you always interrupt when somebody is speaking to you?'

'No, sir, I expect it's me nerves. I'm a little anxious, you see, not having done nothing like this before.'

Mr. Warren stood up and walked over to the fireplace where he pulled a velvet rope which hung down beside the mantel.

'Let us have some tea and perhaps that will steady your nerves. I wish to talk to you about a subject of some importance and cannot tolerate constant interruptions.'

'Thank you, sir.' He was a most considerate gentleman.

'Tell me, before I begin, who is Mary?'

I told him about her, and about Mrs. Marsh and Susan, and he was a good listener and didn't stop me except to question further about Mrs. Watson and her establishment. A maid brought in tea on a tray and the china was the prettiest I had ever seen. There were little fluted cups with sprigs of flowers on them, and the pot and jug were silver, as was the sugar-bowl.

'Sugar!' I exclaimed. 'Why, I haven't seen that since . . . ' I broke off. Since Mother and I went up to the big house, I was going to say, and Cook would often slip a packet into Mother's hands when we departed. But the Cambridge family and the estate were from my past, I had not even told Susan about them. They were a secret, locked within my heart, and nobody was going to learn about that tragedy from me. I did not desire pity, and would gain my revenge, in my own time, in my own way.

'Since when?' Mr. Warren was looking at me intently.

'Since I went with my parents to visit some relations who were richer than us.' I sipped at my tea in an elegant fashion. 'I was brought up proper and knew what to do and how to behave, but it was so long ago now that I've forgotten a lot,' I said.

'Where was your home, Tabitha, before you came to live with the Marsh family?'

'In Hertfordshire, a tiny village, and you wouldn't know the name.' I wiped my mouth with the back of my hand. 'It was years and years ago and then me parents died, fever, it was, and I walked to London and Susan befriended me,'

'You walked to London!'

'And got a lift from a carter for some of the way. It was ever so noisy and dirty and I didn't like it much to begin with but,' I shrugged, 'you get used to anything after a while.'

'And where do you live now?'

I told him about Paradise Court and our one room, and the lack of privacy, and the cold in winter. 'It weren't so bad when Susan was alive because we was earning enough together and I managed to save a bit. But now me savings are gone and I'll never be able to put money aside with three of us to keep on me wage.'

Mr. Warren was silent for a moment, then he began to speak and what he said was so astounding that I was quite speechless.

He wanted to adopt me, to make me his ward, he said, and he was willing to educate me and I wouldn't have to go to bed with him. I was to have my own room and a maid to look after me, and he would engage a governess to teach me how to read and write. And he would arrange for money to be sent to Mrs. Marsh every week so that she and Mary would be cared for.

'Well,' he said, when he had finished explaining, 'why so silent, Tabitha Thomas? It is unusual not to hear you speak.'

'I can't think of nothing to say.' I stared at him, stunned.

'Do you like the idea?'

I nodded.

'Are you willing to give it a try?'

'Yes, but — but why?' There must be a catch in it somewhere. 'Why do you want to do this for me?'

'Because I have more money than I need; because I have no children and this will give me an interest in life; because I have been shocked by what you have told me, and would like to help one family in this wretched city lead a better life.'

'But you don't know me!'

'No matter. I admire your courage and believe that you have enough intelligence to warrant assistance.'

I looked at him doubtfully. 'And payment? How can I ever repay you, sir?'

'Must one always seek reward for everything one does?'

'Yes,' I said firmly. I would never do anything without a reason.

Mr. Warren smiled. 'If I were a religious man I would say it was insurance for the future, a place for me in Heaven, perhaps? But as I am not a believer, let us say simply that I shall gain pleasure from watching you improve and blossom. All I ask in return is loyalty, Tabitha, and the will to better yourself and do my bidding, so that neither my time nor my money is wasted on efforts to make something of you. Do you understand?'

I nodded again. With an education and fine clothes, and a few years to improve my speech and my manners, I could become a lady. My dreams would come true and I would be able to seek out Philip Cambridge as an equal and find a way to avenge my parents' deaths.

'I understand, sir, and thank you. I won't never let you down.'

'Ever,' he remarked, 'and the sooner we start the better.'

I did not go back to Paradise Court but was taken by a maid up to the fourth floor where I was shown into the prettiest pink bedchamber.

The bed had shiny gold knobs on its four posts, which I later learned were only made of brass, but they shone delightfully and made me feel like a princess. The bedcover and carpet were pink, and the curtains were a deeper shade of rose with white stripes on them, and the ewer and basin on a stand by the window were of white porcelain with flowers painted on them. There was a cupboard and a little chest of drawers, and a real looking-glass like the one I had seen at the Cambridges', which could slant backwards and forwards on its stand.

I was left alone until mid-day and spent my time exploring the room and studying my image in the mirror. My eyes were still the same horrid yellow, but they were large and thickly lashed so I could understand Meg's not minding them too much. I looked very white, despite the grime, and my faded velvet was ugly and ill-fitting. I wondered why Mr. Warren should bother himself about me, and who had lived in the pretty room before.

Food was brought up at noon by the

same maid, Daisy, and the beef and vegetables were delicious, as was the little custard tart in a separate dish. I had not tasted meat for years and ate ravenously. Afterwards, a lady arrived who took me shopping. She must have spent a great deal of Mr. Warren's money, for enough dresses and underwear, and bonnets and shawls were ordered for me to clothe a family of six daughters. It was an exciting but rather exhausting business, and when we arrived back at number twelve, the lady, whose name was Mrs. Caroline, told Daisy to bring hot water to my room.

'Have a good wash, dear, and then lie down and rest,' she said. 'Mr. Warren wants you in the drawing-room at six o'clock. I will tell Daisy to waken you at five, so you will have time to dress before going downstairs. Dearie me,' she tutted, 'you will have to wear that gown again until your others are delivered, But give it to Daisy, child, and ask her to brush it over while you rest.'

Having a bath proved to be a most entertaining affair, although that first one was rushed and unsatisfactory because Daisy was terrified of keeping Mr. Warren waiting and would not allow me to linger and enjoy myself. However, after that first occasion I always allowed myself plenty of time for bathing, and my delight in it never faded.

Long ago, back home on the estate, we had brought in buckets of well water and heated it in a large pan on the grange. But after the more recent years at Paradise Court, where it had been almost impossible to wash one's body, my skin seemed to be parched, crying out for the touch of water, and I could not get enough of it.

First of all Daisy would light the fire for me and make sure that the room was really warm, then she would set a towel-horse before the flames, laying towels over it, ready to dry me when my ablutions were finished.

Next, she would pull out the shallow

metal pan beneath my bed, which was painted to resemble wood, and stand it in the middle of the room, with more towels spread upon the floor to protect the carpet. Then a screen was stood against the back to protect me from draughts. Whilst all this was going on I would sit upon the bed, hugging my knees to my chest in an ecstasy of anticipation.

Downstairs Daisy would go and return a while later accompanied by Kitty, both carrying great copper cans of water, one hot and the other cold. They were extremely heavy and the maids had to carry them up four flights of stairs, but they never complained, looking rosy and breathless as the correct mixture, hot and cold, was poured into my bath.

Daisy would then usher Kitty out with the empty cans and assist me to undress. She piled my hair on top of my head and would soap and scrub my back whilst I sung her the songs which Mother had taught me. When I was ready she would bring me the warmed towels and I would be rubbed and dried until I glowed like a beacon. After this all the water had to be carried downstairs again.

I loved my bath nights but dared not ask for them too often because of all the fuss and commotion they caused.

Mrs. Caroline did not live at St. James's Square but came in daily to be my companion. Miss Norton was my governess.

I liked Mrs. Caroline. She was gentle and sweet and came every afternoon, sometimes staying until ten o'clock at night. She reminded me a little of Mother, although she lacked gaiety. Mrs. Caroline always dressed in grey silk, with a lace collar at her throat and a lace and muslin cap upon her soft brown hair. She was gentle-eyed and quiet-moving and I became very fond of her.

But Miss Norton was angular and cross-faced and nothing I did or said was right.

Her dark brown hair was pulled back so tightly from her face that it looked painful, and her skin had a yellowish tinge; so did her teeth. Miss Norton wore dark blue or black dresses unrelieved by any colour or ornament, and her fingers were long and bony and always red. A room across the landing from my bedroom was made into a schoolroom and the governess occupied the small space next door.

It was a very narrow room with but a bed and a chest in it, and she had to use the schoolroom in the evenings as her sitting-room. I did not have much sympathy for her, remembering Paradise Court and the discomfort I had experienced there for so many years. But compared to my bedroom, Miss Norton's was sparse and uncomfortable, and perhaps this was the reason for her bad temper.

Mother had found me difficult to teach in the old days, and now that I was so much older learning my alphabet and numbers was extremely hard. But I thought of Mr. Warren's faith in me, and, gritting my teeth, applied myself to my lessons as best I could.

My mornings of schooling were detestable, but the afternoons were pleasant, for then Mrs. Caroline would take me for walks in the park, or we would go for drives in Mr. Warren's fine carriage and visit places of interest. If the weather was inclement, Mrs. Caroline would read aloud to me as I worked at my tapestry, and it was a great joy to be able to sew for pleasure and not in order to earn my keep.

I washed my face and hands daily, which was another joy, and once a fortnight Daisy would help me to wash and dry my hair which caused almost as much fuss as my bath. She also assisted me in dressing every morning, and whenever I changed my attire during the day, for if I were bidden downstairs to see Mr. Warren, Mrs. Caroline insisted that I change my clothes.

'It's ever so nice assisting you, miss,'

Daisy confided in me. 'Mr. Arnold was always on at me about this and that, but now I scarcely 'as time for 'im. I must see to my Miss Thomas, I tells 'im, every time 'e wants me to do something, and that do annoy 'im, miss!'

I learned that Cook was married to Mr. Arnold, the butler, and that Kitty and Annie shared a room with Daisy in the basement.

Soon after I arrived at number twelve I asked Daisy who had used the room before me. It was a very feminine room, yet Mr. Warren appeared to have no family, and when he did have guests they were always gentlemen who shut themselves away in the library, on the ground floor, and played cards until dawn.

The dining-room, on the first floor opposite the drawing-room, was seldom used, for Mr. Warren dined out mostly, and I had my meals with Miss Norton in the schoolroom during the day, and the evening meal was taken with Mrs.

Caroline in my little sitting-room on the third floor, opposite Mr. Warren's bedroom.

It was a most inconvenient house for the servants, with two rooms on each floor, except for the fourth floor which had my bedroom, the schoolroom, and Miss Norton's poor little box-room all squeezed in together. But when I mentioned this to Daisy she had no complaints.

'Our legs is good and strong, me and the other maids,' she said, 'and I don't mind running up and down stairs. Course, I'm newish 'ere, but the other two got used to it, like, when Mrs. Warren lived 'ere. She were Mr. Warren's mother. *She* 'ad your room, miss, and we're not s'posed to talk about 'er — the master don't like it. But Cook says she were living in that top room for years 'n' years. Then when the old master died she went away and nobody's seen 'er since. A real mystery, innit?'

Daisy and I giggled and chattered

together, and I felt that she was the first friend I had ever had. Susan and I had always been too weary to laugh or have fun, and little Mary had been too young and shy to converse with.

Daisy was even plainer than I was, poor dear, with a sallow skin, boot-button eyes, and black hair scraped back beneath her cap. She was very thin and small but possessed an amazing energy and was always cheerful and good-tempered.

'How did you find work here, Daisy?' I asked her. 'And where were you before?'

'In an 'orrible 'ouse before this, miss, an' I really 'ated it but my old gran — she's gone now an' I do miss 'er — well, she knowed Mr. Arnold, and when saw 'ow unhappy I were in me last position, she 'ad words with Mr. Arnold, and 'e took me on. An' right glad I were, Miss Tabitha, 'cos we get well fed and no one's unkind to us, and now — with you 'ere — I'm real fortunate, indeed I am!'

'Are your parents alive, Daisy?'

She shook her head. 'Ain't got no family, miss. It were only me and Gran, then she went and I'm on me own. But it don't matter too much, not with this work. Cook's ever so kind to me and it's like me own 'ome. I belongs 'ere, miss.' And she nodded and smiled so that I did not feel sorry for her.

But when I thought of little Mary Marsh my conscience pricked me, and I often wondered how she was, and if Mr. Warren had kept his promise about sending money to Mrs. Marsh. I longed to return to Paradise Court and tell them all about my adventures, but when we went out Mrs. Caroline was always with me, and she told me that Mr. Warren did not want me ever to visit my old abode.

I did not see Mr. Warren often, but once a week he would send for me and I would go down to the library. This was an impressive room, with two walls lined with books, and a great mahogany desk set in the middle of the carpet.

Two armchairs were placed on either side of the fireplace and I believe Mr. Warren spent more time in that room than he did in the drawing-room on the first floor.

It was here that he would question me about what I had been doing during the week and ask what I had learned from Miss Norton.

'I do not like her,' I told him. 'She is impatient and cruel and hits my fingers with a stick when I forget things.'

'Then you must learn to remember, Tabitha. For she tells me that you possess a good brain but are unfortunately lazy about using it.'

'I am not lazy! It is only that she goes ahead so quick — I cannot remember all the things she says.'

'Try a little harder, my dear, for you have much time to make up and cannot remain in the schoolroom indefinitely. I want you to learn to ride, and paint, and to study a musical instrument. But these must wait until you have mastered the alphabet.'

My heart lifted at the thought of riding and painting, but it sank again as he finished speaking. I would never be able to read and write, of that I was certain.

'Do not scowl, you look like a spoilt child. Here, look at this book.' Mr. Warren showed me a beautiful leather-bound volume with gold-edged leaves. 'It is called *The Arabian Nights*,' he said, 'and when you can read to me from this book, and copy out one page in your own handwriting, I shall dismiss Miss Norton and you will be freed from your hours in the schoolroom.'

5

Everything went well until I disobeyed Mr. Warren and went back to Paradise Court.

I had long wanted to see Mary again but the opportunity had never arisen. Then, one day the following spring, Mrs. Caroline had a slight fever and could not come for her usual afternoon. Miss Norton announced that I could go for a short walk so long as Daisy accompanied me. There was a cold wind blowing and she had no intention of putting her nose out of doors, so Daisy and I ventured forth and I knew at once where we would go.

'Follow me, Daisy,' I said, excitement welling in my breast, and I led her, breathless and laughing, for we went at a great pace, up to the Strand.

We received some strange looks when we entered the court, for I appeared a young lady of means, and Daisy was neat and demure in her maid's outfit. But I glanced neither to right nor left, holding my breath as the old familiar stench assailed my nostrils, and traversed the dirty yard as quickly as I could.

Daisy puffed up the stairs behind me. 'Gracious me, Miss Tabitha, where are you taking me? Mr. Warren won't like this at all, indeed 'e won't.'

'He won't know, Daisy. Follow me quickly, we don't have much time.'

I flung open the door on the second floor and found myself gazing at the still figure of Mrs. Marsh, seated as usual before the fire. But it was burning strongly, I noticed, and there was a full sack of coal beside the grate.

'So you're back.' She stared at me with her sombre eyes. 'Come to show off, have you? Found yourself a gentleman like our Meg, I suppose?'

'It's not what you think — he's adopted me,' I said quickly. 'Where's Mary?'

'She's sick.' Her mother nodded her head towards the corner and to my consternation I saw a small curled shape under the grimy coverlet.

'Mary, I've come back to see you.' I crossed the room and bent over her. 'What is wrong with you, love? It's me, Tabitha, and I've come to tell you all about my adventures.'

Mary's cheeks were flushed and her brow was hot to my touch. She opened her eyes as I spoke but they were blank, unseeing.

'Have you called the doctor?' I asked sharply. 'What is wrong with her?' Mrs. Marsh's lack of interest annoyed me. 'Do you receive money regularly now?'

She nodded in a listless fashion.

'Then why are there not fresh covers on the bed? Why haven't you bought a carpet and curtains? Why is it all as horrible and wretched as when I was here? You were supposed to use that money to improve this hovel!'

Daisy was standing open-mouthed just inside the door and as her eyes went round the miserable dwelling, the dirt and poverty struck me anew.

'It's my Mr. Warren who sends the money — I asked him to help you,' I cried.

Mrs. Marsh shrugged and huddled closer to the fire. 'Ain't no good,' she muttered, 'I've lost all my children and don't care about nothing any more.'

'For goodness sake!' I left Mary and went across to shake her mother roughly by the shoulder. 'That little girl is still alive but she is very ill and needs help badly. Have you called the doctor to her?'

'Tommy's gone and Susan's gone and Meg don't come no more. It's best if Mary goes, too.' She pulled away from my grasp, her eyes momentarily alive, flashing dislike. 'And it's all on account of you! We were all right till you came — then Susan sickened and there wasn't enough food for you as well . . . '

'But I earned too, and gave you money every week!'

She ignored me. 'Mary began to ail as soon as you left — not been well since then. It's all your fault she's dying.'

'That's not true — oh, how can you say such a thing!' How dared she blame me for the family's misfortunes? I had helped, and was helping still with Mr. Warren's assistance. 'Where do you think the money comes from each week? How did you get that coal?'

'Conscience money,' she sneered, then reached down and produced a bottle from beneath her skirts. She lifted it to her lips and, throwing back her head, swallowed a good portion of the contents. 'Conscience money,' she repeated, wiping her mouth with her hand. 'Paying us off because you've struck it lucky. If you really wanted to help why didn't you get us out of here? And come and see Mary? But you ups and goes and never thinks of us again. Pah!' Her eyes were glazed and she fumbled again for the bottle. 'And now my baby's dying and it's all because of you. Slut! Get out of here and leave us in peace. And see that your fine gentleman pays for the funeral.'

Daisy touched my arm. 'We'd best go, miss. We've bin gone too long.'

'In a minute.' I turned my back on Mrs. Marsh and went across to the bed in the corner. 'Mary,' I whispered, kneeling beside her, stroking her hot little hand. 'Mary, it's Tabitha. Oh, look at me, dearest.'

I willed her to respond, pushing back the wet hair from her forehead. But her breathing was laboured, and although her eyes were open she was delirious and did not know me.

'Daisy,' I turned to the maid in anguish, 'what can we do for her?'

'Nothing, miss, and do come away. It's not right to be 'ere, I'm telling you.' She was holding open the door, anxiety all over her face. 'Mr. Warren's gonna be that angry with us, that I do know.'

'All right, all right.' I stood up, brushing down my skirts, and took one last look at the little girl before following Daisy out onto the landing. I did not look at Mrs. Marsh again.

'I'll speak to Mr. Warren when we get home, I can't leave her like that, Daisy. And I'll tell him to go to Dr. Carpenter and give orders for Mary to have proper attention. That mother of hers isn't going to do anything and it's not right! She'll not suffer any more if I can help it, poor little girl.'

But I did not get the chance to speak to Mr. Warren on our return.

Arnold opened the door to us and told me stiffly that the master required my presence in the library. My heart sank at this summons and Daisy threw me a terrified look as she scuttled downstairs to the basement.

He was furious. He would not allow me to say one word in self-defence but stood, grim-faced before the fire, his hands behind his back.

'You have disobeyed me, Tabitha, and I told you before that loyalty and trust were of utmost importance. You will now go to your room and remain upstairs for one week. You will do whatever Miss Norton demands, and you will receive nothing but bread and water for seven days. As you were so anxious to return to your former abode, such sustenance will doubtless not be too unpleasant. But I will not tolerate disobedience, Tabitha.'

Mr. Warren did not raise his voice, but the very quietness of it, his extreme self-control, was more intimidating than if he had shouted at me.

'After one week you may come downstairs, but should you disobey me again you will be sent back to where you belong and have to make your way in life without assistance from me. Is that fully understood?'

I nodded, wanting to cry from the unfairness of it all, hating the sight of his tall black figure, and the cold dislike in his voice. And what of Mary, poor deserted, doomed Mary Marsh? But I could not beg for her now, not when he was in such a rage. Squeezing back my tears so that he should not see my despair, I hurried from the room.

A week later I was allowed to leave the fourth floor, a chastened girl. Those seven days had been like eternity and they had not been pleasant. I was exhausted and hungry and feeling very sorry for myself. But I had learned all my letters in that time, dinned into my reeling head by the governess, aided by daily abuse from her stick. I could recognise short words and had begun to link letters together in copperplate handwriting. I also knew my tables up to six times twelve.

It was a pleasure to see Mrs. Caroline's kind and concerned face again, but my delight quickly vanished when she informed me that Daisy had been dismissed from service.

'It's not fair!' I cried, on seeing Mr. Warren that evening. 'Daisy only did what I told her and it was right to punish me but she was innocent.'

'We will not speak of the matter again, Tabitha,' he answered coldly. 'I have done what I deemed necessary, now come and read to me. Miss Norton informs me that your progress has been remarkable this week.'

I would not be silenced. My punishment had been accepted without argument, but this was too much. 'What about Mary? She was very ill and I wanted you to send a doctor only you wouldn't let me speak. How can you be so unfeeling?'

'The child is dead,' said Mr. Warren. 'John, the coachman, who takes the money each week, told me of her death. Now, Tabitha, calm yourself.'

I broke down then, not caring that he saw my grief. Mrs. Marsh had been right, if I had not gone away Mary would have got better. I could have made her better, I knew I could!

'Tabitha, stop.'

'You don't understand! It was all my fault — she loved me and I left her without a word, and came here and was given fine clothes and good food, and I never went to see her and now she's gone and I can never make amends.'

I sank down upon the sofa, covering my face with my hands, crying as I had never cried before, not when my parents died, not when Susan Marsh had gone.

Mr. Warren was silent, allowing me to weep. I cried for some minutes, thinking of Mary, and of Susan whom I had not loved enough, and of Daisy, who was perhaps, even now, seeking refuge in a room as cold and as filthy as the one in Paradise Court.

'She has no family — where can she have gone?' I lifted my wet face to stare up at my companion's still form.

'Who?' He looked surprised.

'Daisy. Where has she gone? What will become of her?'

'I have no idea and cannot make myself responsible for every piece of flotsam and jetsam in this God-forsaken city.' His tone was unusually rough and he turned sharply away from me and walked over to the window. 'Tomorrow, Tabitha, I am going away to Paris for a month or so. During my absence you will remain in the charge of Miss Norton, and Mrs. Caroline, who will come and stay in this house with you. If you misbehave, I shall hear of it, and you will then follow Daisy to wherever she may have gone. I care not. If, however, you have worked with diligence I shall see that piano and riding lessons begin on my return.'

He turned from the window, awaiting my reply.

Lifting my head I gazed back at him, then I nodded. I would behave impeccably, so as not to jeopardise the chance he had given me. I would do his bidding, learn all that I could, become the talented, charming, amiable young lady he desired. But deep in my breast I had begun to hate him, to hate his cold, unfeeling soul, his wealth and his superiority.

It was a man's world, I realized, in which women were dismissed or punished, humiliated or petted, according to a man's whim. My mother had been used and killed by just such an arrogant, uncaring wretch.

I, it was true, was being educated and pampered by Mr. Warren's wealth, but it was never to be forgotten that he owned me, directed my life, had total control over me.

One day, I said to myself, mopping at my face and swallowing down the rest of my tears, one day I shall be wealthy too, and so powerful that I will never again say 'Yes, sir' or 'No, sir', or have to do a man's bidding. One day I will be a lady of importance and no one will have control over me again.

★ ★ ★

On the 23 March 1851, Mr. Warren took me to the opera to see *Lucrezia Borgia*.

I was 21 years old then and had achieved the beauty and the elegance for which I had striven so long.

The colour of my eyes did not offend me any longer, indeed I found their amber shade pleasing, as did countless gentlemen of my acquaintance, and Madame Cartier had taught me to dress in a way which showed up their unusual hue.

I wore gowns of ivory tarlatan, cream-coloured velvet and rich golden taffeta; white was not permitted, although I was a young girl, for it did not flatter me; nor did blue or pink. Green was allowed and my jewellery was of the same colouring; emeralds and topaz, and rubies which looked splendid on my cream silks and laces.

My hair had darkened and become very long and lustrous. Sometimes I wore it loose in ringlets, but more often it was coiled into a chignon, or held in a crocheted net at the back of my neck.

I had spent the last two years at a finishing school for young ladies in Paris, and before that one year in Italy, studying art. The Italian family with whom I lived had been warm, voluble and noisy and had made me feel very much at home. But in Paris, Madame Cartier's establishment had been cold and elegant, and the other pupils equally so. However, Madame had taught me everything I knew about gentlemen. She had taught us to flirt in a refined manner and she had given me confidence in myself. I had learned how to make the most of my appearance and how to speak and laugh and move like a well-bred yet desirable young lady.

When I returned to London that spring, I could sense that Mr. Warren was pleased with me. His money had not been wasted and a swan had taken the place of the once ugly duckling.

My shoulders were white and sloping, my waist was eighteen inches when laced and my feet and hands had remained small and narrow. Although there was little of my mother in my outward appearance, my hands must have been inherited from her. One vivid impression of Father, which stayed with me over the years, was his big hands, wide and thick-fingered, yet which were capable of holding a frightened bird with infinite gentleness.

People were not quite sure what to make of me, however, and Mr. Warren did not help them. I stayed at his home, and acted as his hostess on the few occasions when he invited guests to dine. Mrs. Caroline had been reinstated as my companion, and she acted as lady's maid also, but my position was ill-defined in the household. I was neither a daughter nor a niece; Mr. Warren did not refer to me as his ward any longer and it doubtless appeared odd that a young female should dwell in the same house as a wealthy and eligible bachelor.

Sometimes I wondered if Mr. Warren intended making me his mistress; certainly some of his friends, with a wink or nod, signalled that they assumed this was the relationship between us. But Mr. Warren remained coolly distant towards me and I, enjoying his patronage, asked no questions and accepted all that he chose to give me.

That night at the opera Mr. Warren

had taken a box for the two of us, and I knew that my appearance was more than satisfactory. My gown was made of gold-coloured tulle, the panniers edged with a deeper yellow velvet. I wore my long drop topaz ear-rings and my hair was drawn back into a net encrusted with gold beads. My evening cloak was of a rich brown velvet and my fan was ivory, painted with tiny flowers. I saw admiration in Mr. Warren's eyes and felt content, for he was not the easiest of men to please.

For a while I amused myself by studying the crowds who were filling up the stalls below. Then, suddenly, my attention was attracted by movement in the box opposite and I caught my breath in shock.

'What is it?' Mr. Warren had been watching me and he now leaned forward in concern. 'What is the matter, Tabitha?'

'Those people — over there — who is she?'

It was not the lady who had attracted

me, she was small and fragile-looking in a gown of deep red velvet, but it was the man with her.

'That is Mrs. Cambridge, I believe. She is with her husband and I think that is the younger Cambridge with them, I forget his name.'

'Do you know them?'

I knew it was Philip Cambridge; his face had been often in my mind over the years, becoming dim and blurred as time passed, but never wholly forgotten. Never. He was broader, possibly taller, than when I had last seen him — eleven, twelve years ago, was it? But the black hair, the narrow face and arrogant tilt to his head, those had not altered.

So he was married.

I raised my opera glasses and brought his face into closer view. He had not sat down and his features were slightly shadowed, but I could make out his thin nose, somewhat too long, and his stern humourless mouth. His features were not handsome to my eyes, but his air was distinguished and his lean face and black hair, tall figure and haughty stature, were presumably what made females fall in love with him.

I wondered if his wife knew of his past escapades, for my mother had not been his first dalliance, and, remembering his reputation, I doubted that she had been his last before finding himself a spouse.

Poor little wife. She looked small and alone and rather sad, sitting by herself in the front of the box whilst the two men chatted together behind her.

Mark Cambridge had altered more than his brother, but then he had been but a youth of 17 when I had last seen him. Fairer than Philip, with a rounder face, he had soft hair which fell across his brow, and his mouth was wide and looked as if it smiled often.

'Why so interested, Tabitha?' Mr. Warren's voice interrupted my thoughts. 'Would you like to be introduced?'

'No, thank you,' I answered quickly, lowering my glasses. 'The lady reminds me of a girl I knew in France, the likeness is there but I can see now that she is not Bernadette.'

'I was at school with Philip Cambridge. I'll send a note round in the interval, if you wish. They come from Hertfordshire, perhaps you knew something of them in your childhood?'

'Goodness me, Mr. Warren!' I slapped his hand playfully with the back of my fan. 'I was but a poor country girl and could know nothing of such gentry! Do not always seek so hard to please me, sir, or I shall become thoroughly spoilt!'

I smiled at him and made my long ear-rings bob against my cheeks.

'It is nice to spoil you. I still cannot believe that you are the same dirty and impudent little baggage who made my life so difficult a few years back.'

'Impudent? I was never that, sir.' I smiled again and fluttered my eye-lashes, flirting with him as we had been taught to flirt with every male of reasonable status who crossed our paths. 'You quite terrified me!'

His expression changed at my look, and he sat back, his mouth tightening. Thank heavens he was going to be more sensible than the younger men of my acquaintance, who came fawning after every smile, begging for attention after every sally. At least with Mr. Warren I could relax a little and not seek to amuse and entertain every time I opened my mouth.

In France I had learned how to please a man, how to attract and flatter him. But men did not interest me and beneath my smiling mask was a mind with but one aim. I wanted revenge; had harboured it in my bosom for so many long years that the desire had crystallized and I could think of little else.

Whilst I had been away from England the fact had been brought home to me more than ever before that I was an orphan. The other girls had chattered about Mama and Papa, they had all had families and loved ones who visited them at Madame Cartier's establishment on Sundays, and to whom they went during the holidays. Mr. Warren, it was true, came to Paris on a few occasions and I returned to England for the Christmas holidays each year. But I did not really *belong* anywhere, and often wondered what my mother and father would have thought of me now that I was a lady.

Father, I think, would have been quite out of his depth — he knew much about animals and birds and woodland life, but his big ungainly body and slow mind would not have been at ease in a drawing-room. I had loved him, of course, but it was unlikely that we would have had anything in common now.

Mother was different, however, and anger burned in my bosom with renewed fire as I thought of Philip Cambridge. For Mother would have delighted in my success; she, who was so lively and beautiful herself, would have enjoyed my rebirth and I could see her in my mind, taking her place in the sumptuous drawing-room at St. James's Square and looking splendid. Perhaps even making Mr. Warren smile, with her impish ways and ready laughter.

It was all negative thinking on my part, for if Philip Cambridge had not caused her death, I should not have come to London to seek my fortune, and we would all still be living in the gamekeeper's cottage, and I would probably be walking out with one of the labourers on the estate. Nonetheless, I missed my parents still, more now than I had before; there had been little time to think at Paradise Court and at Mrs. Watson's, and less in which to grieve. But now that I had time, and could see how other girls lived, and how happy most of them were with their own families, all the old fury and bitterness welled up within me and peace of mind would not come until I gained my revenge.

I was almost ready for action; now I had the status, the wealth, almost the means to carry out my vow. Seeing

Philip Cambridge again after so long was surely a sign. Somehow I must travel to Hertfordshire and gain entry to the favoured world of the upper classes. I must become acquainted with the Cambridge family and gain access to their home. But not with Mr. Warren at my side. I must go alone, unhampered by his presence. They must have no knowledge of my past, nothing to link me with poor little Tabitha Thomas and her tragic parents. I must become their trusted friend and companion, and then I would be free to do what had to be done.

As the lights dimmed and the heavy curtains swung apart to reveal the stage, the glorious music of Donizetti filled the theatre. But I was lost in my own world, my mind thrusting this way and that, striving for the perfect plan.

6

One evening that autumn I was on my own. Mr. Warren had gone out and Mrs. Caroline had retired early with a headache. She had taken over my sitting-room on the third floor and lived with us now. I, in turn had been given my old schoolroom for a sitting-room, and Mr. Warren had arranged for new furniture and wallpaper whilst I was on the continent. He had chosen my favourite colour, green. And with a Brussels carpet upon the floor, and a green settee with fat embroidered silk cushions; mushroom-coloured velvet curtains, and a green and ivory wallpaper, the bare old room was quite transformed. Yet, despite all the luxuries around me, contentment evaded me and I knew that peace of mind would never be mine until I had fulfilled my childhood vow.

Settling myself at the escritoire, which was also new, I began to write.

Money was the first problem. Like Meg's gentleman friend, my patron never gave me any coins and the only wealth I possessed was my jewellery. But I had plenty of that; precious gems which Mr. Warren delighted in giving me at every opportunity, on my birthday, on my return to England, and most of my new gowns, it seemed, requred some additional piece to set them off.

Sell Jewels, I wrote, and then stopped and pondered. How was this to be achieved? Certainly, several hundred pounds lay within my reach if a way could be found to turn the gem stones into pieces of gold.

Where To Live? That was the next question. With luck, no one in Oakhurst village would recognise me, provided I changed my name. But an abode would have to be found, a small house rented, not too costly, where I could live as a lady of limited means.

A widow! That was it. I would write to the vicar explaining that I had been recently bereaved and sought a dwelling in the peace and solitude of the countryside in order to recover from my grief. We had not been church-going folk, so I remembered the parson but vaguely from that terrible day of my parents' funeral. He was elderly then and might have been replaced by a younger man. But whoever inhabited the vicarage now would surely be a kind and helpful soul, who would deem it his duty to aid a lonely widow.

Get To Know Mrs. Cambridge, I wrote next. Once friendly with her it should not be difficult to gain access to the manor house.

Widow's Garb was the next query. I could sew garments for myself in the privacy of my room; Mrs. Caroline need not be the only female to retire early on account of a migraine. But how to purchase enough black material?

I did not dare to take Mrs. Caroline into my confidence; she was a sweet and mild-tempered lady but she doted upon Mr. Warren and no secret would be safe with her. A pity, for it would not be proper to arrive in Hertfordshire unattended and a maid would be useful for running errands.

A Maid? Could I ask Mr. Warren for a young person to be my personal maid? But that would offend Mrs. Caroline, who looked after me in a satisfactory manner and was a pleasant companion, and too young to be retired.

Drat! I put a hand to my head, wondering how I was ever to achieve my aim. So many obstacles lay ahead that it all seemed well-nigh impossible. I folded the sheet of paper and locked it carefully away in the top drawer of my desk, then hid the key in the toe of one of the shoes I seldom wore.

Two weeks later Fate took a hand in my affairs. I had driven to my milliner's in Bond Street and as it was Mrs. Caroline's afternoon off, Mr. Warren allowed me to travel alone with his coachman of many years standing. On our way home we were held up by a mass of horse-drawn vehicles in Picca-dilly, and I glanced out of the carriage window and saw a girl selling hot chestnuts from a brazier on the pavement. I had not tasted one for many years so I reached up and called out of the window to John.

'Have you a penny, John? I'd love some chestnuts and they would warm your hands while we wait.'

He looked round and grinned, then swung himself down from his seat, feeling in the pocket of his greatcoat. Then he turned and made his way over towards the girl. In a few minutes he was back, thrusting a bag into my eager hands.

'It's Daisy, Miss Tabitha, and she's coming to have a word. I'm not stopping, mind, but it I can't get going yet awhile you might manage a little chat. Don't tell the master, though,' and he winked before clambering onto his seat behind the horses.

'Daisy!' I leaned out of the window as she scurried towards me.

'Can't stay, Miss Tabitha, but oh, 'tis good to see you again!' Her little white face gazed up at me and she looked ill and even thinner than before. ''Ow are you, miss? My, but you're elegant now!'

'Daisy.' I reached out and grasped one of her cold hands. 'Daisy — are you here every day?' My brain began to race, here was the very person I sought.

She nodded. 'Most days, while the chestnuts last. I were lucky to get this work, 'aven't bin too lucky of late, miss.'

'Can you read?'

She shook her head, puzzlement clouding her eyes.

I heard John call to the horses and with a jolt the wheels began to roll.

'Daisy,' I cried, 'I'll be coming this way again, look out for me and do whatever I say. Do you understand? I need your help.'

She nodded, standing back from the gutter, then the carriage gathered speed and her small figure disappeared from my sight.

The next time I saw Daisy I was better prepared and had made my plans carefully. In a small bag I deposited my emerald ring and a pair of gold ear-drops. On Mrs. Caroline's next afternoon off I again visited my milliner, and John took the same route. Once again the traffic was heavy in Piccadilly and I told John to draw to one side and wait for me.

'I won't be long but I have a little present for Daisy and wish to give it to her myself. She has fallen on hard times and it was all on account of me. Now don't be grumpy,' I went on quickly, looking at his dour expression, 'you would be grateful for a kind word, yourself, if you were in her shoes.'

I hurried away down the pavement and saw to my relief that Daisy was there, and alone. No one was buying from her and it took but a few minutes to push the bag into her hands and tell her what I wanted done. Then I was back to the carriage, the door was shut and John was calling to the horses and we were on our way.

I waited seven long and dreary days, then on the seventh evening I bade Mrs. Caroline good-night and retired to my room. It seemed a long time until the clock struck midnight.

Opening my bedroom door I listened carefully, then down the stairs I tiptoed, past Mrs. Caroline's room and Mr. Warren's, on down to the dark hall towards the front door. The bolts drew back noiselessly and I swung the heavy door open. Within seconds a shape moved from the tree-lined pavement opposite and Daisy sped across the road to me.

'Upstairs,' I whispered, 'and not a sound until we reach my room.'

I rebolted the door in case Arnold should wake and decide to check the doors, then we moved silently upwards, freezing at every creak and rustle. But nobody heard us, nobody stirred and we reached the safety of my top floor at last.

'Now tell me,' I said, settling myself upon the bed and patting the space beside me, 'sit here and tell me all that you have done, but keep your voice low.'

'Phew!' said Daisy, blowing out her cheeks and removing her bonnet and shawl. 'It was ever so creepy coming 'ere this late at night. I don't like it, miss, it's scarey!'

'Never mind that, you are safely here now,' I said impatiently, 'and you'll only have to do it once more. Tell me, quick — have you done everything I asked?'

She nodded, sitting down beside me. 'I got a room, miss, nice and respectable like you told me, and I've paid 'em so they won't be asking questions. A married couple with several children, and two other rooms already let.'

'You got the money all right? You had no trouble selling my ear-rings and ring?'

'No.' Daisy shook her head. 'Didn't like 'im, mind, nasty old Jew, 'e were, but 'e gave me a good price so I got the room and the black material. I'm sewing every spare minute, Miss Tabitha, and one dress is almost finished. 'Ere's more of the stuff for you.' She fumbled in her bag and produced a wad of ugly black crape.

'And you bought yourself some decent cloth, I'm glad to see.' I smiled at her neat form. The shawl was warm, the skirt was of a good heavy weave and stout boots encased her feet.

'As you said, miss.' Daisy giggled and reached out to touch my hand. 'I'm ever so grateful, Miss Tabitha, and I eat proper now and keep meself clean. It's a wonder 'aving money in me pocket. But what's it all about, then? I done what you told me but don't know nothing else.'

'I am going to start a new life, Daisy. It will be a grand adventure and I want you to travel with me as my maid.'

'Travel?' Her eyes widened. 'Are we going to foreign parts, miss?'

'No, no! Only to Hertfordshire. And I cannot tell you more except that this is something I have to do, and nobody must guess where I am going. Mr. Warren would be so angry.' I shivered.

He had spent money on me, had made me what I was, had given me a chance in life. For a moment I felt a pang of remorse — it was not kind to use him thus. But then I thought of Mary, yes, and Daisy. Mr. Warren had not been kind to them; he had not considered their feelings, so no more would I consider his.

'I am going to run away, Daisy, because Mr. Warren would never let me go willingly, and I am returning to my childhood home.'

'What! And leaving all this? This 'ouse, and all what Mr. Warren gives you?' She looked at me as if I were mad. Perhaps I was, a little. But this had to be done; I had thought about it, and worried and planned for years, nothing would stop me now.

'But why all in black, miss?'

'Because I must not be recognized and a widow's weeds are a good disguise. Besides, how else can a female live alone? I could not take up residence as a young, unmarried lady, now could I, Daisy? Then people would surely wonder and talk, and gossip is the last thing I want. We must settle down quietly, I am grieving bitterly for my husband, and we will live a secluded existence for a while until the people in the village have accepted us.'

'And then?'

'Leave that to me, Daisy, and do not pry,' I answered sharply. 'I shall pay you a wage and provide you with a home and with food and clothing. That is all you need to know.'

'Yes, miss,' said Daisy.

'Now, can you cook?' After the excellent fare at St. James's Square I had no intention of living off bread and cheese again, and my knowledge of cooking was negligible. Vaguely I could remember Mother's rabbit stews, and her feather-light pastry, but what little I might have learned from her had been forgotten. Madame Cartier had taught us about menus, and what to offer if we had guests to dinner. But it was always assumed that we would preside over a large household and have both a cook and a housekeeper at our command.

Daisy nodded. 'Nothing fancy, Miss Tabitha, but you gives me some veg and a bit of meat and I reckon I kin cope. Seen Cook do it often enough, I 'ave, and her dinners were real splendid affairs, and we was allowed the pickings. I'll be all right so long as you're patient and don't expect too much.'

'Good. Then all we have to do is complete my outfits — I'll get on with another dress here in the evenings, and you finish what you are doing. Then I shall write to the vicar of Oakhurst and ask if he knows of a small house to rent in the neighbourhood.' I put my hand to my mouth. 'Oh! I nearly forgot — I must have a new name. Who shall I be, Daisy? What is your surname?'

'Smith, miss,' and she giggled. 'Don't rightly think that would do for a nice genteel widow lady, would it, miss?'

'No, Daisy, I want a more distinguished name — let me think.'

'Me gran's name was lovely,' said Daisy, after a pause. 'She were Emma Moon. How would that do?'

'Mrs. Moon? Yes!' I sat up straight and beamed at her. 'That will do famously. I'll be Mrs. Moon and my husband was Clemence — how delightful! Now,' I went on more seriously, 'I still have plenty of jewels left, so that should keep us for several years and we can sell off pieces once we are there.'

'Several years? You planning to stay that long, Miss Tabitha?'

'I've told you not to question me, Daisy. If you do not wish to accompany me, then say so at once and I'll look for somebody else.'

'Oh, no miss, I'll come. But it seems ever such a long way away — never bin out of London before — and it will be ever so strange at first, won't it?'

'It will be an adventure, Daisy, and you'll be better off than you've ever been before so I don't know why you are worrying.'

'I'm not worrying. Just thinking, like.'

I was thinking, too, and wondering what would happen to me. Daisy was innocent and would always be able to find work afterwards. But what would become of me?

Philip Cambridge must die, on that I was determined. But the way in which he would meet his death was not yet decided. Somehow, it must appear natural, for I did not intend being arrested for his murder; all that had been achieved during the past years was not going to be thrown away by me now. I was young and had many years before me to be enjoyed, once vengeance was mine.

I shook myself free of doubts and fears and brought my mind firmly back to the present. It was arranged that Daisy would visit me once more in a month's time for the final arrangements, then I led her downstairs and she slipped away into the night, bearing with her a brooch and my topaz necklace.

Two weeks later Mr. Warren called me down to the library and told me that Mr. Steven Arnott had asked for my hand in marriage.

Mr. Arnott was a pale-faced, fair young gentleman, who blushed easily and who had escorted me to the theatre on a few occasions. I knew that he was interested in me, but this was not remarkable, for many of Mr. Warren's friends regarded me with interest.

'Well,' said Mr. Warren, after his announcement, 'what have you to say?'

'I do not know Mr. Arnott well,' I replied slowly, 'at least, I have spoken but a few words to him.'

'He is the eldest son of Sir Archibald Arnott and does not lack for money. He has few brains but is not unkind, I think, and is considered an eligible bachelor by those who know about such matters. He tells me that he wishes most ardently to make you his wife, although he cannot know you very well, either.'

'How can a gentleman be sure of loving a girl whom he scarcely knows?'

'He has fallen for your pretty face, my dear. Do you not find it a compliment that such a worthy gentleman should be willing to wed with a girl from the slums?'

I hated it when he threw my past at me and spoke in that disdainful manner.

'I do not believe it matters if one is brought up in a palace or a pigsty, sir! What does matter is good manners and a consideration for the feelings of others.'

'Well said, Tabitha. I am put firmly in my place. You would be wasted on young Arnott, who, I hasten to add, knows nothing of your background. He possesses neither your intelligence nor your courage.'

I bowed my head at this praise, wishing that he might always be rude and unpleasant — how much easier it would be to leave him if I hated him all the time. But sometimes I was quite fond of Mr. Warren.

'Why do you have such a poor opinion of my sex?' I asked, raising my head to look at him.

He had never mentioned his parents to me and I should have liked to have known more about his mother.

Mr. Warren's face stiffened and he turned away from my gaze. 'That is a long and painful story and not one I intend relating to you. Do I take it that Mr. Arnott's attentions are not desired, and his feelings not returned?'

'That is correct, sir. Now, if you will excuse me I shall go to my room.'

He nodded, allowing me to depart. There was still an abundance of sewing to do and time was passing quickly. As I hurried upstairs my brain began to work feverishly. I must leave soon. If Mr. Warren were to begin match-making, it would not be long before he found some eligible gentleman from among his friends, to whom he would like to see me wed. And once he had settled on someone my liberty would be even more curtailed and escape might well prove impossible. How fortunate that he had not taken it into his head to marry me himself! For I was so beholden to him and he was such an obstinate man, it would be difficult to refuse him.

Mr. Warren was such a moody and strange man; I did not always understand him. Perhaps it was because there was nobody close to whom he could talk. He had undoubtedly had an unhappy love affair and thus regarded all females with distaste. Once I had gone, maybe he would turn to Mrs. Caroline, herself a widow. She was a sweet lady, who adored him, and she was the very wife for him if he would but see it.

In the New Year a letter came from the vicar of Oakhurst, saying that he knew of a small house which could be rented and that he would be pleased to make arrangements for me with the local agent. Daisy brought the letter with her, for I had given him that address, and within two months we were both safely ensconced at The Vista, in Oakhurst village.

Daisy had escorted me to her room one dark night in March, we had hired a carriage the following morning and we were out of London and swiftly away within a few hours.

Notes had been left for Mrs. Caroline and Mr. Warren; it had been difficult to know what to write — to Mrs. Caroline I had said simply that I was going away, that I had been happy with her and she was in no way to blame for my departure; she would always be remembered with affection.

Mr. Warren had been more of a problem. What could I say to the man who had rescued me from dire poverty, given me a home and an education, raised me to the status of a lady and spared nothing to make me beautiful in both mind and body? What excuse could I give for my extraordinary behaviour, without letting him guess my true intentions? So I gave no reason for my leaving. I thanked him for all that he had done for me and asked him to forgive me. There was nothing else to say.

The village had changed since I had last seen it, but possibly my childhood memories were blurred by time. We had lived two miles out on the Cambridge estate in my youth and I had always thought of Oakhurst as a place of many people and many houses. But after the London streets it was an oasis of calm and appeared to have shrunk in size. It was so quiet, too. At night there were no sounds save for the occasional barking of a dog and the hooting of an owl.

Daisy felt very insecure at first.

'It's ever so quiet, miss, and nothing's going on. Whatever are we going to do with ourselves?' She stared at me, her black eyes very round in her white face. 'Who we going to talk to? You won't never leave me 'ere on me own, will you, Miss Tabitha?'

'Now, Daisy, don't be foolish,' I replied, 'and don't call me miss. I'm Mrs. Moon now and a grieving widow — don't forget.' I removed my hideous black bonnet and gazed around the front parlour.

There was this room and a kitchen at the back, from which ladder-like stairs led up to two small rooms beneath the rafters. The front steps opened straight onto the road, but there was a garden at the rear and a privy hidden behind a yew hedge.

The rooms were clean, with white-plastered walls, and we decided to live mainly in the kitchen which was warmed by the range. There was a rack of iron pans and skillets upon the wall, and a cupboard filled with plain but serviceable china. Off the kitchen was a small scullery, with a copper and a wooden tub for our laundry. There was a well in the garden and a plentiful supply of coal for the range; one oil-lamp and a great many candles.

The vicar had arranged for a woman from the village to come up and prepare the house for us, and although the furniture was sparse, it was dusted and tidy and the linen was adequate for our needs.

'We may stay here for a year, with the option to remain for longer, if we desire it,' I said cheerfully. 'We have got to keep the house clean and go shopping, cook our meals and wash our clothes. We will go to church on Sundays and you will doubtless meet people when you go shopping, Daisy, so listen to all the gossip and tell me everything you learn. I am particularly interested in the Cambridge family, who live in the manor house and own most of the land hereabouts, so keep your eyes and ears open.'

'Dearie me, I don't rightly know what's going on, I really don't. And what'll we do when the money runs out?'

'You've never worried about the lack of money before,' I said sharply, 'so don't start now. I still have some jewellery left and over two hundred pounds in my bag, so do not fret. Let us get something to eat and then we'll wash and go to bed. We are both tired and everything will seem much better after a night's sleep.'

★　★　★

I first saw the Cambridge family on our first Sunday in Oakhurst. Daisy and I had walked to church early, for I wished to observe the congregation as it came in. Shortly before the service began, there was a rustling and murmuring and then everybody rose to their feet and bowed and bobbed as the Cambridges passed down the aisle.

Daisy was all agog beside me.

'Who are they?' she whispered. 'Ain't she pretty? Are those all 'er children? Now 'e's a real smart gent!'

I shoved my elbow into her inquisitive little body and she subsided with a muffled squeak.

Through my veil I saw the same pensive little lady whom I had seen at the opera, leading two young girls and a boy down the aisle, followed by Mr. Philip Cambridge. My brain worked rapidly as I wondered which of the girls was my half-sister. The older one, surely? She must be about 12 years old, the other about 8, and the boy somewhere in between.

Who were the other children? Mrs. Cambridge did not look to be much older than me, although her air of sorrow added maturity to her pale face. But it was the eldest girl who caught at my attention — she was beautiful. Shiny black ringlets hung beneath a blue velvet bonnet, and the same rich material encased her slender body. Her head was demurely lowered as she went past, but I saw the sweep of very long eyelashes and the suggestion of a dimple in one rosy cheek. She did not look at all like me, but I could not see the colour of her eyes.

The family walked to the front of the

church where the Cambridge pew was situated, and as they all seated themselves, the girl turned to look up at her father and her face was radiant as she smiled at him.

She was exquisite and I hated her; hated her for living while my mother had died, hated her for causing my father's death, hated the way she so obviously adored the selfish, uncaring brute beside her.

God help me, I prayed, knowing that it was wrong to think thus, yet feeling wretched and helpless against their wealth and well-being and united strength. I had to ask for extra help to aid me in my task ahead. God help me to avenge my parents' deaths. They died because of him. And her.

When the service ended the Cambridge family went out first and spoke a few words with the vicar on the porch steps. Then we lesser mortals followed, and as the Cambridges were climbing into their waiting carriage, it seemed to me as if the little wife turned her head and looked straight at me.

She was the one I would have to get to know, for she held the key to the manor.

Two weeks later a note arrived from the lady.

The vicar has told me of your sad loss and I realise that you won't be visiting for a while. But life must be lonely for you, Mrs. Moon, and I wondered if you would allow me to call on you very briefly, on Wednesday afternoon? Please tell Hubbard if this would be convenient. Yours, in sympathy, Sylvia Cambridge.

I agreed, of course, and Daisy and I spent hours polishing and cleaning and dusting; taking out and washing the best teacups and saucers and tidying the already spotless front parlour which we never used. Daisy baked some rather hard biscuits and I sliced bread very thin and buttered it, before cutting it into neat pieces. Then I told

Daisy to answer the door to our visitor and not appear again until I rang for tea.

Sylvia Cambridge was as sweet and gentle as she looked, reminding me somewhat of paintings I had seen in Italy, of sad-eyed madonnas. She was clad in a gown of soft green, which made me very envious. It was full-skirted and heavily flounced, with wide sleeves ending just below her elbows; white sleeves of muslin were beneath, gathered in at her wrists. She wore an over-jacket of white embroidered muslin, bordered with lace, and the dearest little green bonnet was perched upon her dark hair. Emeralds were in her ears and one square-cut green stone adorned her left hand. The entire outfit would have suited me to perfection and there I had to sit like a dowdy crow in my black crape.

'I know a little of what you must be feeling, my dear Mrs. Moon,' said my visitor softly, 'for I lost my father three years ago and still have not recovered from the loss. We were very close, you see.'

'Clemence died almost a year ago,' I replied, 'but I still miss him greatly; that is why I came to live here. It is a fresh start with no memories. Perhaps life will be easier in the country.' I lifted my black-bordered handkerchief to my eyes, unable to dislike her despite her appearance, she was so genuinely sympathetic.

'You must get out of that dreary black,' Mrs. Cambridge leaned forward and patted my hand, 'it is so dreadfully melancholy. As soon as the year is up you must begin to wear lilac and silver grey. Oh, not very pretty, I know, but a pleasant relief after that horrid mourning. And you are young, Mrs. Moon, and must try to be cheerful and look ahead. Life has not ended for you and there will be many happy years ahead of you, I'm certain.'

I nodded, looking down at the black material which covered my form. It was ugly and did not suit me at all, but it was useful for the moment.

'Have you lived here long, Mrs. Cambridge? Tell me about yourself so that I may forget my troubles.'

'I have been at the manor for just over two years. My husband brought me here as his bride in the spring of 1850.'

'Then those are not your children?' I exclaimed.

'No.' She lifted her chin. 'They are my husband's. Have you any family, Mrs. Moon?'

I shook my head, wishing that she would continue to talk about herself. 'I am an orpahn and Clemence had but one brother who is in America.'

'America? Then one day you must meet Mark, my brother-in-law. He went to America last year to seek adventure.'

'I should like that.' Hopefully, Mark Cambridge would not return for many years. He might well remember me better than his brother, and I was uncertain as to how good my disguise was, or how much I had changed since childhood. I had met nobody yet who had known me in my youth. Daisy had recognized me — but then she had seen me grow into a young lady during the early years at St. James's Square. My first test would be with the servants at the manor. Some of them I had known well by sight. Which of them still remained, I wondered. Later on, when I knew her better, I must ask Sylvia Cambridge about her household.

'I am not ready for entertaining yet,' I went on, 'but in a few months, perhaps I shall feel able to face the world.' And I lifted the handkerchief to my face once more.

'Of course, Mrs. Moon, do not distress yourself.' Mrs. Cambridge tutted to herself in a flustered manner and then began to talk about other matters.

Whilst we had tea she told me about Miss Trundle, her dressmaker in Hertford, to whom she would introduce me at a later date, and she told me of her love of riding, and hoped that I would join her on horseback in due course.

'We have a large and beautiful estate and there are many places to ride, Mrs. Moon. I shall enjoy showing someone around for I am lonely, too.'

I did not question her further about this statement. Why should she be lonely with all her money, and a husband, and those children to care for? But when she left she promised to visit again soon, and I looked forward to further acquaintance with Mrs. Sylvia Cambridge. She was a most agreeable lady and far too nice for that husband of hers.

★   ★   ★

'Them's all Cambridge bastards,' Daisy remarked, a week or so later, dumping her basket of groceries down on the kitchen table and taking off her shawl. 'I 'ad a real good chat to a woman what works up at the big 'ouse, and she weren't in no 'urry so we nattered good and 'ard, me being new 'ere and wanting to know all about the local gentry, like.' She winked and nodded.

'Good for you, Daisy.' I wiped my hands on my apron and went to sit down at the table. 'What else did you find out?'

'That eldest, Miss Primrose, she's 'is favourite and a right spoilt miss *she* is. Dumped on the doorstep as a tiny babe, she were, real story-book fashion, and 'e's doted on 'er ever since. And Mrs. C. don't like 'er, so they say, and can't do nothing with 'er. The other two came along later . . . '

'Dumped, too?'

'Well, he ain't a bad man but was real wild in 'is youth, so 'e's trying to make up for it now. Nobody knows who the mothers are but 'e's admitted to fathering them, and 'e's giving them an 'ome and an heducation. They're being brought up proper, like you was with Mr. Warren, miss.'

'Madam,' I said sharply. 'And Mr. Warren was not my father and had no feelings of guilt about me, so he was a good man and took me in out of the kindness of his heart. Mr. Cambridge is not kind, Daisy, he is simply doing his duty by those misbegotten children. And what of the women he seduced and then abandoned? Has he done right by them?'

'I don't know, miss — madam — and there's no need to go shouting at me so. I'm only telling you what I 'eard. But they all think a lot of Mr. C. and what he done for those youngsters. Managed all on 'is own for years, 'e did, with nurses and the like, then 'e marries to give them a proper mother and that poor Mrs. C. can't cope, it seems. Folk don't like 'er, madam, but they all like 'im.'

'I like her,' I said. 'She's kind and sweet and gentle and those children are probably a lot of spoilt brats. Poor little lady, no wonder she looks sad. I am sure they make her life miserable and resent her presence.'

'That Miss Primrose were ever so upset when her pa married.' Daisy nodded. 'Fair crazy about 'im, she were, and then this new wife come along and she's not so important any more. Though it seems as if she is number one again now, and Mrs. C. is being put to one side. Too weak, they say, no strength in 'er, and why 'asn't she produced an hair? A rightful hair, that is. Bin married more than two years now and no sign of a baby.'

I first went riding with Sylvia Cambridge that autumn of '52 and we both enjoyed ourselves so much that it became a weekly occurrence provided the weather was fair. She showed me all over the estate that I had once known so well, and on one occasion we rode down to the woods and saw my old home.

It was derelict now, crumbling into ruin, and I stopped my horse, my heart sinking at the desolate sight.

'Who lived there?' I asked, a lump in my throat and my eyes smarting from unshed tears.

There were no crisp white curtains at

the windows, and the front door sagged half-open on broken hinges. Mother's garden had vanished under brambles and long grass, and the well was overgrown, the rusty bucket lying on its side, half-concealed by a bed of nettles.

'It used to be the gamekeeper's cottage,' answered Sylvia, 'but now Wilson is housed at the other end of the woods. I believe there was some tragedy years before I came here — my husband does not like to speak of it — but the couple died who were living there, so I've been told, and nobody wanted it after that. Unlucky, they said, or some such nonsense. It has not been inhabited for a very long time.' She tugged at her horse's reins and turned its head out towards the open field. 'Come, Mrs. Moon, the sight is distasteful to me — I cannot abide anything ugly or broken, can you?'

So it was on his conscience, was it? I touched my mount lightly with my whip and turned to follow my companion. And well it might be! Two lives destroyed because of him, and a child missing, or dead. Did he remember that there was once a little girl, whom he had called a brat, and whom his brother had kissed? Probably not. It seemed unlikely that so proud a man would remember a child. But his conscience had smote him so that he had taken in his bastard daughter and given her a life of luxury, thus paying for his sins. But not quite enough. Mr. Philip Cambridge would have to pay more dearly for his past actions before I had finished with him.

I had not met him yet. Sylvia and I rode frequently together, she came to my house often, and I had been up to the manor once for a brief visit, to take tea in her charming sitting-room. There, I had seen no one apart from the butler, who was new, and a little maid who had brought in the tea things. I was not ready for a more social life and intended living quietly for a while longer. But my friendship with Sylvia Cambridge was growing stronger with every passing day, as was her need of me. I was content to watch and wait.

7

How strange it was to be walking through the front rooms of the manor house, whilst my mind clung to memories of the back stairs, the sewing room set high up beneath the attics, and the warm kitchen where Mother and I were given cups of tea before going home.

I remembered the kitchen well, it was a big cheerful room, warmed by an immense grange which was fitted with ovens and boilers and put our poor little affair at The Vista to shame. There was a magnificent display of copper pans and skimmers and sieves of various sizes hanging beside it, and a deal table in the middle of the flagged floor, with a deal dresser filled with china against one wall. Two Windsor armchairs stood in front of the grange, for the sole use of Cook and Mr. Knowles, the butler.

Much had changed in the big house, but the cook I had known was still there, stouter and greyer, yet looking remarkably like the cook of my youth. So much so that I did not go often to the kitchen, fearful of recognition. Fanny, I remembered vaguely, but Molly was new, as were the two kitchen maids. Bates, the butler, had left, which pleased me for he was the link between Primrose and myself, and a different man now attended to Mr. Cambridge's needs and lorded it over the other servants. Mrs. Ryan, the seamstress, had retired also, I learned, and for this I was thankful. She and my mother had been very friendly and apart from her possibly recognizing me, I could not have borne to see her again and be made to remember those far off days of my innocent childhood.

Now I was a grown woman, with an overpowering ambition, and it was reassuring to know that there were but few remaining servants who might remember me.

We had managed very well, Daisy and I, for a year or so, but then she became fond of the local butcher and I could see that she would not be with me for very much longer. William was a big, red-faced, lumbering lad with scarcely a brain in his head and a heart of gold. Daisy wound him round her little finger and he used to gaze at her small sallow face and angular little figure as if he had never seen anything so delightful in all his life. They were right for each other and I knew that William would care for her and love her as she deserved. But if they should decide to marry what would become of me?

My other worry was lack of funds, for although we sold the rest of my jewellery and lived quietly and frugally at The Vista, bills had to be paid, and we had to eat, and keep the fires and lamps lit.

One afternoon Sylvia arrived unannounced and found me weeping. Within minutes she had found out the reason for my distress, and before that year was out I was living at the manor as her friend and companion, and Daisy had gone happily off to marry her William.

The arrangement suited both Sylvia and myself, for I had at last achieved my aim, and she had found an ally and was more able to stand up to her tiresome family with my support.

Dear Sylvia did not love her husband but she loved me. For the first time since I had been orphaned, I felt loved. Susan Marsh was kind to me, but affection was hard to show or feel in Paradise Court, and little Mary clung to me because of need, especially after her sister died. But Sylvia loved me in a warm and generous way, giving me endless presents, laughing at my feeble jokes, listening to me talk with an interest which was delightful.

'Oh, Tabitha,' she said often, 'You are the sister I never had. You have time for me and you are strong and honest and such fun to be with. How did I ever manage without you?'

I was given a bedroom just down the passage from Sylvia's bedchamber on the first floor, and most of the day we would sit together in her downstairs parlour. This was much smaller and cosier than the drawing-room, and we could be on our own there, away from the rest of the family.

Soon after I went to live at the manor, Sylvia began whisking me into the town of Hertford to visit her seamstress. There I was measured and fitted for new gowns which seemed to please my companion as much as it pleased me. Three new day dresses were chosen, of brown and green shades, made of worsted poplin and trimmed with darker bands of velvet. I also ordered matching bonnets made of velvet and silk.

Sylvia enjoyed spoiling me and I was so thankful to be out of my miserable black crape that I cared not for convention and refused any mention of grey or lilac. My companion also directed that two tea-gowns should be made for me, my favourite being of green again, with black buttons and braid trimmings, and white under-sleeves and a darling white lace collar.

The children were often insolent to their stepmother and at first I could not understand why she allowed such behaviour.

'I want them to accept me, can't you see that, Tabitha? They resent my presence — after all, they were here first. And for Primrose it must be especially hard. Although, heaven knows, she has little to fear, Mr. Cambridge shows her far more affection than he does me.'

'How did you first meet your husband?' I asked, wondering why, with all the likely brides he could have chosen, Mr. Cambridge had chosen meek little Sylvia.

'At a ball,' she answered, smiling her wistful smile. 'He knew my dear father previously, they had always got on well, and Father liked Mr. Cambridge and decided that he was the right man for me. I was an only child, you see, my mother died when I was very young, so Father and I were particularly close. He wanted the perfect husband for me — I think he realized then that he was dying — and after knowing Mr. Cambridge for some time he announced that he was the one.'

'Did he not know of Mr. Cambridge's reputation?' I bent over my sewing, hoping that she would not think me impertinent. I had never queried the three children's presence in the household.

Sylvia also stared down at the needlework in her hands and her voice faltered. 'Father told me only that Mr. Cambridge had had a wild youth and had behaved impetuously and foolishly as a young man. But now that he was mature he had settled down and become a country gentleman of sound views and impeccable manners, he said. Father did ask me if I found him pleasant in appearance and of course I did. What girl would not?' She lifted her head and spoke more firmly. 'Philip Cambridge was the most eligible bachelor in these parts and the most handsome gentleman that I had ever seen. There was also something most romantic about his — ' she hesitated — 'his dashing past.'

'Did you know about the children then?'

Sylvia shook her head. 'Perhaps he was not quite honest with me. But we had a happy few weeks in Italy after the wedding, and it was only on our return to Hertfordshire that he told me about them.' She sighed. 'I have tried so hard, Tabitha, wanting them to accept me. But I am unused to children and do not know how to handle them.'

I thought of freckle-faced Edward, with his swagger and impudent smile; his blue eyes, so wide and innocent, and his cruel hands.

A few days before I had caught him torturing a kitten behind one of the barns.

'You wicked boy!' I cried, pulling the

limp body from him and striking at his red curly head with my fist. 'How dare you torment an innocent creature in such a way!'

I held the soft body against my breast, willing it to live.

The boy shrugged, his mouth curling in contempt. 'There are plenty more where that came from, so you can't stop me, Mrs. Busybody Moon. The moment your back is turned I shall find another and do with it what I will.' He stuck his hands in his pockets and sneered at me. 'This is my home and I belong here. You do not.'

My bosom heaved with anger. 'I shall tell your father of what I have seen and you will be punished.'

Edward laughed. 'My father won't listen to you — your job is to look after that silly wife of his. You are not my keeper and should mind your own business.'

I turned away, stroking the soft fur of the little animal, willing it to show some sign of life. But it was beyond help, perhaps fortunate not to suffer any more. Not looking at the boy again, I went in search of Hall, the gardener, and together we buried the kitten beneath a sycamore tree.

Hall was old and gnarled and gruff. But he was a countryman and there was a gentleness about his big hands as they dug the tiny grave, which reminded me of Father.

'Young limb,' he muttered, bending over his spade, 'ain't natural to go round hurting defenceless creatures — there's a bad streak in him though the master don't see it. Your pa wouldn't have stood for such behaviour, that's for certain.'

'My father?' I stared at his bent form, feeling the blood drain from my face. 'What do you mean by that, Hall?'

'You don't deceive Jeremiah Hall, not one whit.' He straightened and leaned on his spade, his faded blue eyes gazing at me with mild curiosity. Over his corduroy breeches he wore a stained and grubby smock, and his greying whiskers were in need of a trim. Yet despite his shabby appearance there was a dignity about the old gardener which appealed to me. 'Young Ben Thomas and me,' he said, 'we growed up together and I seed your parents wed, and you as a young 'un, running all over this place here. I knowed you, Tabitha Thomas, the moment I set eyes on you again.'

'Don't say anything.' I clasped my hands before me. Feeling so safe with the house servants, I had forgotten that there were others who might remember me. I, certainly, had no memory of Hall, yet I trusted him. 'The past is over and done with,' I said, 'and I have made a new life for myself and do not want anyone to know about me. Do you understand? I am Mrs. Moon now, and the Cambridge family accept me as that.'

He nodded soberly. 'Ain't none of my business what you're doing here. Sad about your folks, though. I missed your pa, I did. We had some good chats in the old days and things ain't the same no more. Young Wilson's all cocky and know-it-all — they aren't made like Ben these days.' He shook his head gently, then shouldered his spade and began to move away from me. 'You keep your eye on that young 'un,' he muttered, 'got a nasty streak in him, I'll be thinking. The missus ain't got no control and the master don't want to know.'

'I'll try, Hall,' I called after him, 'perhaps his father needs telling the truth about his beloved son.'

★　★　★

I had seen little of Mr. Cambridge since coming to the manor. He had met me briefly on my arrival and had informed me of my yearly wage, as companion to his wife. He had not shown any interest in me, and seemed thankful that his wife was pleased with me, and that I would keep her happily occupied. He had certainly not recognized me. But to my eyes he was little changed; abrupt and arrogant as ever, he treated his wife in a barely civil manner and wasted what affection he possessed on his bastards.

I did not take my meals with the family but had trays brought up to my room on the first floor. However, shortly after arriving at the manor, Sylvia began joining me in my room.

'They would rather be on their own,' she said, 'and I would much rather be here with you. It is understood that if we entertain I shall of course play the part of hostess, but if only the family are present my appearance is neither necessary nor desired.'

'You are running away from the battlefield,' I warned. 'It is a foolish thing to do and will get you nowhere.'

'I have fought for nearly four years, Tabitha, and have achieved nothing. Do not preach, I beg, but say that you will have me here. You are pleased, are you not?' She gazed anxiously at me. 'I will not force my presence upon you if you do not wish it. You have enough of my company all the rest of the time.'

'Dear Sylvia, do please sit down. Of course I am glad to have you here with me. But for your sake I do not think it a wise move.'

'That matters not! I am going to do what I want from now on, it will make a pleasant change. Oh, Tabitha, I am so glad you've come.'

If she had known what was in my mind she would not have said that. But I did not believe that Sylvia Cambridge had any feelings left for her husband, so if I gained my revenge it should not cause her too much distress. And she was so lost, so helpless in the midst of that uncaring family, it would be a pleasure to champion her against the rest of the Cambridges.

Primrose was the eldest and she bore a likeness to my mother which infuriated me. Her eyes were the same dark blue that I remembered and her skin was white and without blemish, although her hair was darker than Mother's had been. My mother's had caught the light when the sun shone on it, showing up little strands of gold during the summer months. But Primrose's was a deep glossy black with no hint of lighter brown. She had the same vivacity, though, and Philip Cambridge's face lit up when his daughter entered the room; he reacted in the very same way as Father had done in Mother's presence. So added to my dislike of the girl was the even deeper emotion of jealousy.

Thoughts and memories which had been stored at the back of my mind over the years came strongly to the fore now that I was back in Hertfordshire, back in the county, and amongst the people, of my childhood.

Although we were half-sisters, I felt no affection for Primrose Cambridge. My feelings were of strong dislike, even hatred, and the antagonism was mutual. Although the girl could be charming, and had a fresh, appealing manner with those whom she wished to impress, she was spiteful and rude to her stepmother, as she was to me.

'We do not want you here,' she told me, coming into my room a few weeks after I had arrived. 'Father's wife has never been accepted here and neither will you be. Silly Mrs. C. must remain, I suppose, because she is Father's wife. But you are not important and we are going to make certain that you do not stay long.' She gave her dark head a toss. 'It is no use running and telling tales, either, because Father only listens to me and I shall deny everything you say.'

'What a charming family you are,' I answered. 'For a bunch of bastards you are remarkably confident of your place in the household.'

'How dare you!' Primrose sprang forward, thrusting her face into mine, her nostrils arched in fury. 'Don't you ever dare to call us names again, Mrs. Moon, or you'll regret it. We don't like strangers in our house, and we particularly don't like *you!*'

'I can assure you that the feeling is mutual. Now, if you don't mind I would like some time to myself. Kindly remove yourself and shut the door behind you.'

It was foolish of me to have made an enemy of Mr. Cambridge's spoilt eldest daughter, but I hated her for more reasons than she could know and could not hide my feelings.

The following morning I was summoned to her father's presence and quickly became conscious of the fact that I would have to change my tactics. It was also obvious that I would not be able to mention his son's brutal behaviour, either.

'My daughter tells me that you have been both insolent and hurtful in your manner towards her.' Mr. Cambridge was standing in the drawing-room with his back to the fireplace. His hands were clasped behind him, his shoulders were hunched forward and he looked very angry indeed. 'Let me assure you, Mrs. Moon, that I can find a half-dozen ladies to be companion to my wife, so do not delude yourself into thinking that your services are indispensable. My children are very precious to me and I will not have them upset in any way. Is that understood?'

'Yes, sir.' I bowed my head so that he should not read the expression in my eyes.

'They require neither admonition, criticism, nor chastisement from you, Mrs. Moon,' his voice went on, grating on my ears. 'They have a governess to whom I pay a salary for doing just those things. Your task is to occupy and amuse my wife.'

'Yes, sir,' I said again, when he paused.

'Then I want it understood that if I hear one more word of complaint from any of the children, you will be out of here, Mrs. Moon, and on your way to Timbuctoo for all I care.'

'I apologise for what I said to Miss Primrose.' The words almost stuck in my throat. 'It will not happen again.'

'Then guard your tongue well. I have no use for interfering females in my house.'

'Yes, sir.'

When he dismissed me I went up to my room, so full of anger that I dared not face Sylvia, not until I had gained control over my emotions.

How dare he speak to me in such a fashion? He, who had assaulted, seduced and probably raped more girls than he would ever remember; who had produced heaven alone knew how many illegetimate children; who treated his wife in a most contemptible way; who paid more attention to his rude and ignorant bastards than he did to Sylvia Cambridge. He, who had caused my mother to die, and my father!

He dared to preach at me and threaten me with dismissal if I spoke the truth about his daughter. Bah! One day I would get my own back.

Gripping my bottom lip between my teeth I paced my small room, my breast heaving with wrath and indignation.

But this was no way to go about my plan — I must not annoy him, for it was imperative that I gain his interest and then his affection. Madame Cartier's teaching had been sound and I was certain that I could make any man find me attractive. But I must go about things the right way, and had begun badly by antagonising Primrose, and therefore her father as well.

Sitting down on my bed, I thought deeply on the subject and ignored Sylvia's bell the first time it rang. But then it rang again and I dared not leave her alone any longer. My work had to come first for the moment, my plan would have to wait awhile before it could be put into operation.

The next few weeks were a testing time, indeed, for both Primrose and her brother went out of their way to annoy and frighten me. I discovered live frogs in my bed, a heap of writhing earthworms in my washbasin, and, on one occasion, the skirts of two dresses were ripped and the lace collar ripped from my favourite tea-gown.

No complaints, he had said. Very

well, I thought, and remained outwardly impassive aware of the children's curious glances and furtive whispers and giggles, yet allowing no shadow of emotion to play upon my face when they confronted me.

'Did you sleep well, Mrs. Moon?' Edward asked sweetly, the morning after I had discovered the frogs in my bed.

'Thank you, yes, I had a most restful night,' I replied, smiling at his innocent face.

But after my clothing was ruined I had a quiet word with Hall, and a day later he sent a lad to see me, who fitted a new lock to my bedchamber door and gave me the key to it. Then I saw Molly, one of the maids whom I had grown to like and trust, and I told her to come to me for the key whenever she wished to clean my room.

I did not say a word to Sylvia, or to her husband, and went out of my way to smile at the children, or to nod pleasantly, whenever I saw them. They, somewhat disconcerted, must have decided to leave me in peace for the time being, and with relief I turned my attention to Harriet, the youngest.

She had tried to be rude to me, spurred on by the older two, but she was only 10 years old and needed loving as badly as little Mary Marsh had done. Indeed, she reminded me greatly of Mary, for although she was well fed and well clothed, she was pale and thin, with wispy fair hair and the same haunted eyes. I wondered why Sylvia had not sought her affection, for she was a dear little thing once I got to know her.

I began going up to her room every evening to tell her a story before she went to sleep, and before Primrose and Edward, who were allowed to stay up later, retired for the night. I always tucked her in and gave her a good-night kiss. Miss Graham, the governess, did not bother with her after she had had her supper and been sent to bed, and she was a very lonely child.

'I haven't got a mama,' she told me one night, looking small and lost in her big bed. 'Prim and Eddie say it doesn't matter because we have Papa, but you can be my mama, if you wish. I like you, Mrs. Moon.'

'And I like you, sweetheart,' I said gently, smiling down at her. 'And even if I'm busy during the day I shall always come up to tuck you in at night.'

Harriet wriggled happily. 'I'd like that. I'm so glad you've come to live with us, Mrs. Moon.'

It was a joy to hear those words after the behaviour of the other two children. Unfortunately, I had not reckoned with Sylvia's jealousy.

'You should not spend so much time with that child,' she scolded, after I had come in from a walk around the grounds with Harriet. 'You are employed to be my companion, Mr. Cambridge says so.'

'But you were not feeling well and did not fancy a walk,' I declared, 'and I was away for less than an hour. I thought you would be lying down and would not miss me.'

'I want you here at my side,' she insisted stubbornly, 'even if I am asleep. Miss Graham is there for the children.'

'Miss Graham may be a clever governess but she is not fun to be with.' In fact, the angular lady reminded me of Miss Norton, whom I could never remember without a shudder. Little Harriet needed to run and skip and laugh, and Miss Graham was not the sort of female whose company one could enjoy.

'Well, do not go out with that child again, Tabitha, or I shall have to complain about you. And I do not want to do that, dearest.' Her tone became wheedling. 'Please do not be offended but think of me. I am so lonely without you and cannot bear you out of my sight for any time at all.'

Sylvia Cambridge was beginning to irritate me. At first I had enjoyed her affection and constant companionship, she had provided the loving attention which had been so lacking in my life. But now her possessiveness was becoming intolerable and I realised that soon her clinging arms would ensnare me forever.

She had few friends and relied on me to provide amusement all day long. I read to her and sewed with her, we talked and walked together, and went riding several times a week. But I quickly learned that Sylvia possessed little intelligence and could think of nothing except herself and her imaginary ailments. After listening to her moans and groans for weeks on end, Harriet's lively companionship was pure joy and I escaped with the child whenever I could. But Sylvia did not like me out of her sight for long, so my freedom was severely curtailed. By the autumn of 1854 I had had enough and decided to start on my plan of action.

One night in October, I remained with Sylvia until she slept, then I went to my own room and prepared for bed.

I put on my long white cotton night-gown, with its ruffles at neck and wrists, and brushed my hair until it gleamed in the candlelight. Then I placed a warm yellow shawl about my shoulders and waited to hear Mr. Cambridge's footsteps on the stairs.

He did not share a bedroom with his wife. Indeed, they had slept apart for the last year, so she had informed me, and he occupied a large bedchamber further down the passage past my room. The children's bedrooms were beyond in the west wing.

Leaving my door ajar, I listened, clutching my shawl across my bosom with one hand, the other holding my candlestick. The moment I heard him begin his ascent I left my room and walked quietly down the corridor towards the west wing, pausing only when I had rounded the corner of the passage and was out of sight.

Then, allowing my shawl to fall open, and hoping that the candle lit my features to advantage, I came back round the corner just as Mr. Cambridge was about to enter his bedroom.

'What the devil!' He turned as he saw me, his brows drawn together, his hand falling away from the door knob. 'Mrs. Moon! What are you doing up at this hour of the night?'

I paused, catching my lower lip between my teeth. 'Beg pardon, sir, only I heard Harriet cry out and was afraid that she was having one of her nightmares.' I lowered my lashes in embarrassment, aware of his searching gaze, allowing my breast to rise and fall in feigned confusion. 'I like to comfort her, you see, she is a very loving little girl who is rather lonely.'

'Lonely?' His frown deepened. 'How can that be? Does she often suffer from bad dreams?' He did not appear in any hurry to send me back to bed.

'I believe her sleep is often disturbed.'

'But why? She is well cared for, well fed and clothed, what ails the child?'

'I do not believe that she feels

wanted, sir. She needs more loving and attention. Miss Graham, if you'll excuse my boldness, is not a very affectionate lady, although she is an excellent teacher, I have no doubt.'

'So you would spoil the child, Mrs. Moon?'

'Not spoil, sir! I do not think that loving has ever spoilt anyone. And Harriet is very young still — she needs a . . . ' I stopped abruptly.

'Needs a mother?' He grunted. 'My wife does not care for children and I have done my best, Mrs. Moon, but must admit that small children are difficult. Primrose and young Edward are more to my liking.' He looked at me in silence for a moment, and I was aware that his glance was taking in every inch of my scantily clad body. 'You gave me a false impression Mrs. Moon,' he said at last, 'with your impertinent manner and interfering ways I had not realised that you possessed a heart.'

'I have a heart, sir.' Lifting my eyes I

looked straight at him, allowing my lips to curve in a half-smile. Then I lowered my head quickly and tried to blush. Madame Cartier had been insistent on our practising this act, it disarmed the most hardened gentlemen and proved our innocence. But I had not blushed for a long time, and without tight lacing it was well-nigh impossible.

Mr. Cambridge cleared his throat and turned back towards his door. 'Yes, well, er — Mrs. Moon, I am delighted that you take such an interest in my youngest daughter, and am grateful for all that you are doing for my wife. Perhaps we can discuss all this at length another time. It is late now and you'd best go to bed.'

'Whatever you say, sir.' I gathered the folds of my shawl about me and moved behind him to walk down the passage to my room.

'How long ago was it that you lost your husband?' he called out behind me.

'Three years ago, sir.'

'And you grieve for him still?'

I looked back at Mr. Cambridge in the candlelight. 'I miss him, but time heals all wounds, sir.'

'Then I cannot imagine that you will be alone for very much longer,' he remarked softly, 'you are a very beautiful woman, Mrs. Moon.'

I smiled and our eyes met and held for a moment. 'Thank you, sir, you are most kind.'

He nodded, then turned abruptly and disappeared into his room shutting the door behind him.

As I climbed into bed, highly satisfied with my night's performance, I wondered fleetingly what it would be like to sleep with a man. I had faced the problem with Mr. Warren and had steeled myself for the worst but there had been no need to fear him. I had grown into womanhood untouched and unharmed. Madame Cartier had taught us much in the way of pleasing a man but she had never ventured further than discussing mere flirtations. The chaste

187

kiss, the hand-clasp, the ardent phrases, these had all been explained to us, but I was uncertain as to what went on in a bedroom between man and wife, although we had all had our own theories in France and had imagined and surmised amidst bursts of giggles and squeals of dismay.

Mr. Arnott was only one of several young men who had made me feel desirable, but none had done more than squeeze my hand and whisper foolish words in my ear. Now I was seeking the advances of a man who was a known philanderer, and I was afraid. But his wife did not love him so I should not be hurting her, and it was necessary for me to become close to him, to have his entire confidence, before I could carry out the rest of my plan.

8

I became Philip Cambridge's mistress on the twentieth of November, 1854, and left his room feeling sore and degraded.

The act of love had been far more distasteful and painful than I had imagined, but fortunately, my dislike of the man had given me courage and I was able to comply with his demands and then return to my room with reasonable dignity. And I had pleased him; this was essential, and the relief at my success helped somewhat to soothe my aching limbs and bitter thoughts. Had my mother enjoyed lying in his arms? Or had he taken her against her will, assaulting her with his ferocious masculinity? I would never know. But the thought of her made me determined to go on accepting his caresses, no matter how much I hated them, and him.

There had been only one moment of real panic once I had forced myself to accept his hands on my body and his mouth on mine. It had been at the end of his lovemaking, when I had hoped that it was all over and he would allow me to return to my room.

'There is one small matter, Mrs. Moon,' Mr. Cambridge said suddenly, turning towards me again and placing his hand on my throat. Then he forced my head round towards him and his voice was rough. 'You were never married, my dear, and I do not like liars.' His hand tightened on my neck making it difficult for me to breathe. 'Well, what have you to say for yourself? Why the pretence, Mrs. Moon?'

He let go of me, lifting himself up onto one elbow, and by the light of the candle I could see his eyes glinting.

I swallowed. 'A female cannot live easily on her own, not without provoking gossip and curiosity, sir. That is why I assumed a married name and pretended to be a widow.'

190

'Where is your home then? Why did you seek an abode in our small village?'

'My father wanted to force me into marriage with a man whom I found repugnant.' The words came quickly, thoughts racing through my panic-stricken mind. 'It was only when I met you, sir, that I realized love could be a pleasurable thing.'

'Indeed!' He laughed and I was able to relax. 'Well, you pleasure *me*, Mrs. Moon, and that is all that matters now. Get away with you.' He slapped my thigh lightly and then rolled away, pulling the bedclothes over him. 'I will let you know when you are next to come to my room. And not a word, if you please, to my wife. I know that you and she are close to each other, but this remains our secret.' He lifted his head and watched as I pulled on my night-gown and draped my shawl around my shoulders. 'The servants may guess and gossip — let 'em! But my wife and I will continue to live our little farce, so guard your tongue, my

191

dear, or you will indeed be sorry.'

'Yes, sir, I understand.' I padded barefoot to the door and let myself out into the corridor.

For the rest of that night I lay in a tight ball of self-loathing and in the morning I washed myself carefully all over. It was not going to be easy, this masquerade, for Philip Cambridge was no fool, apart from being a connoisseur of female charms, and he must never guess how much I hated him.

Sylvia was blissfully unaware of the nocturnal events in her husband's room and remained as clinging and sweet as she had always been. Mr. Cambridge ignored me on the few occasions when we met, apart from asking about his wife's health and general disposition.

But Primrose, I think, guessed at what was happening. She became quieter, more watchful, whenever I was in the same room as her father, and she spoke to me in a restrained manner, even if there was no one else about. She was not sure how to assess the situation and had decided, it seemed to me, that although enmity was felt it was best kept hidden in case of any future development.

Edward, too, had become more polite, so that I had no reason to complain of him. But I saw Hall out in the garden one morning and told him to keep an eye on the boy.

'Tell the other servants that if any of them see him hurting an animal, they are to tell you at once and then you must inform me,' I said.

The old gardener touched his cap but his eyes did not meet mine. 'Yes, m'm,' he grunted, and turned away.

So he knew, too. I watched him go, feeling both ashamed and resentful at his scarce-concealed contempt. If only I could explain to him, if only he could be made to understand my actions, he would not condemn me. But perhaps he would. I was being deceitful, was constantly lying and was planning murder in my mind. Would the simple and honest old countryman condone that? Unaccustomed to feelings of shame, I shook myself free of guilt and walked briskly back to the house.

It did not matter what the servants thought, or said, about me; they were insignificant. What mattered was my plan, my future and the fulfilling of my vow. Nothing must deter me from my aim; nothing and nobody.

One afternoon in May, Mr. Cambridge announced his intention of going to London for a few weeks.

Sylvia and I were sitting in the drawing-room taking tea together, when he joined us. This was an unusual event for if he was at home in the afternoons, he liked to sit in his library, and the children remained upstairs, only coming down to see their father after five o'clock. By this time Sylvia and I had departed to her little parlour where we spent the evening, and the children amused themselves with Mr. Cambridge in the drawing-room until it was time for bed.

'Will you have some tea with us,

dear?' Sylvia was flustered. 'I'll ring for another cup at once and then you can join us.'

'Thank you, madam, I am not thirsty.' Mr. Cambridge's dark eyes rested on me as I sat quietly, hoping that he would go away. It always disconcerted me to be in the presence of husband and wife at the same time, and I hated the way in which he looked at me, possessively, appreciatively, as if he could not wait for the night to have me in his bed again.

At first he had been distant in his manner towards me, but of late he had been careless, as if not caring whether Sylvia guessed about our relationship or not. It placed me in a most awkward and uncomfortable position and I knew that soon I would have to decide on the final plan. Not murder — it would be revenge; retribution for my parents' deaths. But I had not, as yet, found the perfect solution and, loathing him as I did, was fearful that he might guess my true feelings.

'I am not staying,' Mr. Cambridge said abruptly, 'but came to inform you that I intend visiting London at the end of this month for a lengthy stay. Perhaps a month or so.'

My heart leapt and I hastily raised my cup to my lips to conceal my delight at this news. A month, possibly two, without his presence; time to enjoy the solitude of my bed, to be free of his voice, his face and the feeling of his hands upon my shrinking body.

'Oh,' said Sylvia, looking put out. 'I do hope we can manage without you. I do hope — ' she hesitated — 'that is, do be sure and give instructions to Miss Graham, I really cannot be held responsible for the children, you must see that . . . '

He interrupted her, lifting his hand with an air of irritation. 'I intend that you come with me, my dear Mrs. Cambridge, so do not fret yourself, I beg. And the children will be adequately cared for in our absence, we have servants enough for that.'

'Oh, but Tabitha!' Sylvia looked across at me with piteous eyes. 'I cannot manage without my dear Tabitha.'

'Fanny is just as good as me,' I said hastily, putting down my cup. 'She can arrange your hair even better than I can. Do not worry, Sylvia, dear, and think what a nice holiday it will be for you.'

Time for Harriet, I was thinking, time to be natural and to have fun with her for a while.

'You are to come too, Mrs. Moon.' Philip Cambridge's voice rang out with stern authority. 'My wife cannot manage without your attention, so will you both see your seamstress and order what clothes are necessary for the visit, and be prepared to depart from here two weeks from today.' He turned on his heel and left the room.

I was stunned and Sylvia exultant.

'There! What a kind man he is, to be sure. Sometimes I misjudge him. And we will have a lovely time, dearest Tabitha, and we will ask Mr. Cambridge to take

197

us to the opera and to the theatre. Oh, indeed, I am quite ecstatic!'

I could not go. He would have to be told. It was quite impossible. What if I were to see Mr. Warren? What excuse could I give for running away? And what would he say to Mr. Cambridge? He would tell him all about my past, and my employer would quickly put two and two together and he would then know who I really was, and might even guess my reason for returning to Hertfordshire.

Old Hall was a slow-minded countryman, but Philip Cambridge, with his knowledge and guilt, might well wonder why Tabitha Thomas chose to return to the estate where her parents had died, and return, moreover, leaving a life of wealth and comfort behind her, in order to worm her way into the Cambridge household. *And* in disguise, furtively, secretly. Why had I not come openly, speaking of my past and my memories? No, there were too many unanswered questions, too much that was dubious about my intentions. Nobody must ever know who I was.

'Are you not pleased, Tabitha?' Sylvia was smiling and fluttering behind the silver teapot, her cheeks pink with excitement. 'Why so down, dearest? Do you not want to go? Why, London is the most enchanting city with so much to do and see there. You must be happy, and we'll visit Miss Trundle and get ourselves fitted out with new gowns, for we must not appear dowdy coming up from the country.'

'The country suits me best,' I said. 'I love this estate and the leisurely way of life. The idea of crowds and carriages, and noise and confusion and dirt, does not appeal, I must admit.'

'But you'll love it, I know you will! And at least we shall not be pestered by the children and will have a lovely time just on our own. Thank heavens you are here, Tabitha, and Mr. Cambridge did not insist on Primrose accompanying me. How I should have detested that!'

That night I told Mr. Cambridge that

I did not wish to go to London.

'It will not look right,' I said, pulling on my wrapper in readiness to leave for my own bedchamber. 'Sylvia will want me always at her side, and it will look most strange for a paid companion to be attending theatres and going about in extravagant gowns. She is intent on ordering the most frivolous clothes for me, sir, and it will cause unpleasant gossip and will not be seemly. Take Primrose with you. She is longing to go, and is old enough to appreciate such a visit.'

He reached out and grasped my hair, which lay loose upon my shoulders. Then he pulled me down across the bed so that I had to lie on top of him.

'You will come, Mrs. Moon.' His face was very close to mine and I fought off repugnance, turning my head away from him.

'You are hurting me,' I whispered.

'We will say that you are her sister.' His breath was hot against my ear. 'Nobody there knows her history, she is such a dull little mouse, and I wish to see you dressed, Mrs. Moon. Dressed in the most expensive fabrics, dripping with gems. I want to show you off, to make other men envious of me and what I possess. Primrose has plenty of time ahead of her in which to go gallivanting around town. I want you with me this time.'

His hand twisted in my hair, bringing my face round to his, then his mouth closed on mine and I was sickened all over again by his violent embrace.

'I am going to take you to places you have never dreamed of, Mrs. Moon,' he said thickly, 'and you are going to be so beautiful and so alluring, and so damnably seductive, that the fellows will be green with envy!'

'But my father,' I said desperately, 'I might see him and he will force me to return to him and . . . '

'Mrs. Moon,' replied my employer harsly, 'you are no longer a young girl under your father's domination. You belong to *me* now and must do as I say.

Pack your bags and prepare yourself for the journey, we are all going to London, Fanny too, for I shall have need of her. So no more foolish excuses, if you please.'

★ ★ ★

Mr. Cambridge rented a house in Chelsea, close to the river, and although the view from the front windows was pleasant, the smell was not, and we had to make sure that all the windows were kept closed at all times. Fanny came with us, but the house servants and the cook and butler were engaged with the house.

I had journeyed up to the city with my employer and his wife, my thoughts in turmoil, quite certain that I should see Mr. Warren, and I felt faint at the thought. Fortunately, Chelsea was some distance from St. James's Square, but if we visited the theatre, or some other place of amusement, it was more than likely that we would see Mr. Warren.

And as he and Mr. Cambridge knew each other they would be sure to converse.

At first all went well and my fears began to subside; Mr. Cambridge took us to the races and we had a splendid picnic on Ascot Heath. Sylvia and I sat in the open carriage, with our parasols up to shield us from the sun, whilst her husband attended to our wants from the lavishly filled hamper. I enjoyed watching the crowds more than the horses; the tipsters and the acrobats, the gypsies and the shifty-eyed pick-pockets. Fortunately, we sat above the riff-raff, so that we could observe without being jostled and shoved. It was noisy and exhilarating and I had to agree with Sylvia that it was a lovely day and she was so glad that we had come.

Mr. Cambridge also took us to the Cremorne Pleasure Gardens in the King's Road. These had originally been the private gardens of Lord Cremorne, he informed us, and we were pleasantly surprised by the green lawns and the trees and flowers.

We saw a firework display, and a medieval tournament, and a marionette show, and I was beginning to relax and feel safe amongst the crowds when I became separated from Mr. Cambridge and his wife and looked about me a little perturbed by the folk pressing in on all sides.

Although there were many well-dressed couples about, there were also some less attractive people, and some of the women had painted faces and clung to their male companions, laughing in loud and boisterous fashion.

Suddenly aware of a very strong perfume, I glanced at the woman next to me, who was on the arm of a top-hatted gentleman with a very red face. They were watching the marionette show behind me and the woman's shrill laughter and overpowering perfume made me flinch and turn away.

Where was Mr. Cambridge? I looked in vain for his tall figure. The woman beside me shrieked again and then knocked against me as she gesticulated towards the puppets.

'Lord, Charlie, don't they act real? That one reminds me of your snooty-faced ma!'

I looked at her in distaste as she clung to her companion, and then my mouth fell open in astonishment. Less lovely, grubbier and fatter — it was nonetheless Meg Marsh.

I was staring so hard that she became aware of my look and turned to face me.

'Something wrong with me appearance, is there, ducky?' she asked, her painted eyebrows disappearing into the tight frizz of curls on her forehead. 'Haven't you got no manners, lady?' She adjusted her frightful little hat. 'Or wasn't you brought up proper, like me? *I* was always told it was rude to stare.' She hiccuped and swayed, taking a firmer grip on her companion's arm, and I realised that she was intoxicated.

'Forgive me.' I lowered my eyes and

turned away, my heart thudding with shock.

Meg Marsh! Once so beautiful, sunk to this level. And her gentleman, if I remembered correctly, had been named John. What had happened to him? Had he broken off the attachment? She had certainly changed a great deal since those days at Paradise Court. To think that I had once wanted to be just like her!

'One minute.' I felt her hand on my arm and as she pulled me round to face her, I saw recognition flare in her puffy eyes. 'Dear God in Heaven, it's me little friend grown up and all hoity-toity! You're Tabitha Thomas, aren't you, ducky? I remember you. Well I never!'

She was shaking my hand, pumping it up and down with a vigorous movement. 'Here, Charlie,' she called over her shoulder, 'this is an old friend of mine what used to live in the Court with me ma and little sister.'

I tried to back away, desperate to be free of her and all the questions she would ask. But she would not let go of my hand, and her companion loomed behind her.

'Pleased to meet you, ma'am.' He bowed awkwardly, his breath heavy with fumes as he peered down into my face. 'Always pleased to make the acquaintance of any friend of my Meggie's. Care for a drink?'

He straightened and looked vaguely around for a refreshment stall.

'Thank you, no,' I said quickly, 'and I'm afraid I must leave you now and join my companions.'

'Aw, but you can't leave us now, not now that we've met again after so long. Ain't your gown lovely, dearie?' Meg put out a hand and fingered the material of my skirt, her eyes darting over my body, taking in every inch of my form and apparel, an envious smile on her loose lips. 'Done well for yourself, haven't you, Tabs? Tell me — did you find a gentleman friend like you wanted? How come you speak so nice and look a real lady? Did he set you up proper?'

Her eyes suddenly filled with tears and she groped for a corner of her shawl and wiped her nose.

'Funny, innit? You've gone up and I've come down.' She sniffed. 'My John, he got fed up with me and found himself another fancy woman. I had an awful time at first, Tabs, specially being used to a nice house and all them clothes and everything, but luckily . . . '

'Mrs. Moon!' Mr. Cambridge's voice rang out behind me and I felt his firm grip on my arm. 'Whatever are you doing here? We thought we had lost you. Come along at once, Mrs. Cambridge is waiting.'

'Ooh! He's a real swell,' said Meg loudly, as I turned to follow my employer. 'You done well for yourself there, Tabs, but don't forget a friend in need.' Her voice rose, floating after us as we made our way through the crowds to where I could see Sylvia standing. 'I'm at 17 Drury Lane now, dearie, and could do with a bit of help now and again. Don't forget me, Tabs, I've bin kind to you in the past.'

Mr. Cambridge hurried me along, his hand like a vice on my arm, and we did not speak until we reached Sylvia.

'Oh, dearest Tabitha, we thought you'd gone!' She fluttered against me, her little hands patting at me with nervous movements. 'There are some most undesirable people about at this hour of the evening and I was so worried about you.'

'We have already made the acquaintance of one,' remarked her husband brusquely, and pushed us ahead of him towards the main gates. He was in a bad mood and Sylvia, after a quick glance at his set face, lapsed into silence for the rest of the drive home.

When we reached the house, Mr. Cambridge told Fanny to assist his wife to bed.

'I want a word with you, Mrs. Moon,' he said to me abruptly. 'Into the drawing-room, if you please.'

My heart sank as I followed him.

What could I say? How explain my unfortunate meeting with a female such as Meg Marsh?

'Who was that creature?' His tone was harsh as he stared down at me. 'How do you know someone like that?'

'She was someone I knew a long time ago. I — er — helped her at one time because I felt sorry for her,' I said stiffly.

'Do not lie to me, madam. I heard her say that *she* had helped you. Out with it — where did you first meet her?'

When I did not answer he frowned and began pacing the long room, his hands clasped behind his back.

'It occurs to me that we know very little about you, Mrs. Moon. You told me a romantic tale once, if I remember rightly, about your father wanting you to marry a gentleman whom you disliked. I wonder . . . ' He broke off and turned, his black brows drawn together in thought. 'Yet there was no doubt about your innocence when first I took you to bed. You had never known a man before.' He let out a small exasperated sigh. 'Who are you, Mrs. Moon? You defy me with your silence and I should rid myself of you forever. Yet I find you so damned tantalizing I cannot let you go!'

I stood mute before him, holding my head high. Let him think what he would. There would be no explanations from me.

'You will not speak? Very well. Who cares about your past, or where you met that wretched female? We have rid ourselves of my good wife, so tonight, Mrs. Moon, you and I are going out and you shall learn more about the pleasures this great city has to offer. Go up now and change into something more suitable. But pray, do not disturb Mrs. Cambridge. Dress quickly and then come downstairs and join me here.'

'Dress?' I stared at him. It was close on midnight and I was weary. 'I am tired, sir, and would like to go to bed.'

'And so you shall, so you shall.' His

mouth twisted and my heart lurched at the knowledge in his dark eyes. 'But first we must go out, Mrs. Moon, and I want you to look ravishing. Your green taffeta gown, if you please. Get one of the maids to help you, and hurry.'

That night Mr. Cambridge took me in a hired carriage to the Haymarket. The streets were swarming with bawds and prostitutes and I remembered my first meeting with Mr. Warren and realised how fortunate I had been to meet an honourable gentleman in such a place. As the carriage slowed I saw women with young children, both girls and boys, who were offering their little ones to passing men. Harlots were clustered in all the doorways, lifting their skirts and exposing their breasts, desperately trying to gain attention, to earn a few pence for the night.

I shivered and turned to look at my companion who sat silently beside me.

'Where are we going?' I was tired and depressed, wondering what was to become of me.

It had been easy to hate Philip Cambridge, to allow the hatred to harden and strengthen over the years, to vow revenge and plan continually for that end. But how was the deed to be done? I had gained his trust and a place at the manor, but what would happen now? He was far stronger, more powerful, than I. How could a weak and defenceless female ever hope to raise her hand against him? And, moreover, commit the crime without being accused of the deed?

I had allowed myself to live in the Cambridge household, using their wealth for my own satisfaction, enjoying the fine clothes and the good food which Sylvia so generously bestowed upon me; had allowed myself to be used by Philip Cambridge for his own pleasure and had done nothing.

But now I had to think again, now, after seeing Meg Marsh after so many years, I realised how easy it would be to sink to her level, for once Mr. Cambridge tired of me, as he surely would, what would become of me? Having once been the mistress of one man I was doomed, and would continue to be used and abused by other men until finally being cast into the gutter, forced to make my living as these prostitutes in the Haymarket did, going out nightly to earn a few miserable pence to keep themselves from starving.

Why, oh why, had I not stayed with Mr. Warren in safety and luxury, remaining under his patronage as a lady of quality? My stupid childish vow was my undoing and now I was beginning to regret every minute of the last four years and my silly, thoughtless flight away from St. James's Square.

'Where are we going?' I asked, numbed by fatigue and futile regrets.

'You will see.'

Mr. Cambridge called to the coachman to stop, then I was helped down from the carriage and ushered into a lighted doorway held open by a footman, very smartly dressed in white silk breeches, a green jacket and silver buckled shoes.

We were escorted by him up to the first floor where we entered a magnificent drawing-room, hung with crystal chandeliers and filled with a great many people. A strange kind of drawing-room, I thought doubtfully, for there were lots of small tables and everybody appeared to be eating and drinking, served by footmen carrying silver trays. There was a deep-red carpet upon the floor and heavy red velvet curtains covered the high windows. Then it became obvious to me that despite the air of opulence and the good clothing and appearance of the men, all the females were high-class prostitutes and courtesans.

This was a brothel, albeit a superior one, and the madam was a hard-faced, handsome woman in rustling black taffeta, who greeted Mr. Cambridge with a delighted smile.

'My dear man,' she said, sailing towards us through the crowd, her beringed fingers outstretched towards him, 'how nice to see you again. It has been some time since you were last here. Been keeping yourself amused in the country, have you?' She glanced sideways at me with speculative eyes. 'You sure got yourself a little beauty this time,' she said, her red lips smiling. 'Where did you find her?'

I held myself stiffly erect, wondering what was going to happen, hating Philip Cambridge all over again for what he was making me suffer.

'You must allow me to have a few secrets,' answered my companion smoothly, 'but I am glad you approve of my taste. She is a choice morsel, is she not?'

We dined on oysters and caviare, washed down by champagne. At least, Mr. Cambridge dined, I sipped at my wine, watching the oddly assorted gathering, praying that I would not see Mr. Warren's tall figure amongst the assembled gentlemen.

'Seen anyone else you know?' queried

my companion, looking at me above his raised glass. 'You look magnificent tonight, Mrs. Moon, but can you not smile? I find that sulky expression ill-pleasing.'

'I am tired.' I stared back at him without expression.

'Then drink some more — here, give me your glass. You should be grateful, Mrs. Moon, there are not many females of your position who are treated to these luxuries. Are you not hungry?'

I shook my head, wondering where the night would end, wondering when we would return to Hertfordshire, wondering for how much longer I could bear to put up with this loathsome pretence.

Some minutes later the madam appeared again and leaned over Mr. Cambridge, her full bosom almost falling out of her tightly buttoned gown.

'I've given you the usual room and here's the key. Enjoy yourself, and don't stay away so long another time.' She winked at him, touching his face with her finger, then she straightened and with a flick of her skirts swayed away to another table.

That night was the hardest I had had to bear in Philip Cambridge's arms. The champagne and the tawdry atmosphere of the brothel no doubt helped to bring out the worst in him. He abused my body without mercy and I was sickened by his demands. I felt cheap and degraded and near the limit of endurance.

Once we are back in Hertfordshire, I said to myself, willing my mind to think about that and not what his hands were doing to my body, once we are back I am going to kill him. For my poor dead parents' sake, for my own sake, Philip Cambridge must die.

9

By the time we returned to the estate two weeks later, I knew what I was going to do and my plan seemed foolproof. But I had to beware of Primrose. She had not forgiven her father for making her stay behind with the younger children and she blamed me for his action. And rightly so. No doubt if I had not come to the manor, Mr. Cambridge would have taken his eldest daughter to London and played the part of a perfect father, escorting his wife and daughter to the opera and to the races; going out about his own business late at night when his women-folk were in bed.

Primrose was my enemy, although she tried to hide her feelings, knowing that what I said now would hold weight with her father. Yet her eyes said it all, those great blue damning eyes, which she had inherited from Mother, and I would have to be very careful.

Should Mr. Cambridge die, and the circumstances appear in the least suspicious, his daughter would take the greatest joy in denouncing me. His death *must* appear natural — I had no intention of following him to the grave. My life must continue as before, filled with comfort, as Sylvia's friend and companion. If I could bear it. But bear it I must, for there was no other future ahead of me, and Sylvia would always make sure that I wanted for nothing. So her aimless chatter and her aches and pains and little anxieties would have to be borne for ever more. A small price to pay, surely, for release from her husband's tyranny, and the knowledge that my parents' deaths had finally been avenged.

Soon after our return to Hertfordshire Primrose's mind was taken off me, and her jealousy and anger abruptly ceased, for Mark Cambridge returned from America.

He returned to England, tall, sun-browned and very much a man and she was completely captivated by him. I remembered him as a thin, gangling youth — apart from that one brief glimpse of him at the opera when I was with Mr. Warren — and could see little of the young lad I had once known in this handsome man of some thirty-three years.

He was a charmer, with an easier, more open manner than his brother, and he soon had all the females in the household falling over themselves for his attention. Even Edward warmed to him, for Mark would spend time with the boy, playing cricket and ball games, which the boy's father never did, and showing him how to fashion bows and arrows from hazel wands.

One afternoon Mark Cambridge waylaid me as I was coming down the stairs into the hall.

'May I accompany you on your walk, Mrs. Moon?' he asked.

He was wearing tight-fitting yellow

trousers with a dark brown, waisted dress-coat, and a shirt of fine white linen under his embroidered waistcoat. He sported side whiskers and a small blond 'Imperial' and I could understand why Primrose had lost her heart to him. But I did not want his company. So far my plans had been going well, nobody had recognized me apart from old Hall, and I was beginning to hope for a speedy solution to my problems. But now here was someone from the past, someone, moreover, who had known me as a child and kissed me. I still remembered that sticky embrace in the meadow and the laughing, boyish face of young Mark Cambridge. He could be a danger to me; even if he did not guess at my identity, it would be difficult to accomplish my scheme with him in the house.

I hesitated as he smiled down at me. 'I was going to look for Harriet — she normally comes with me at this time.'

'Harriet is busily occupied in the kitchen helping Cook to make biscuits for our tea, and my sister-in-law is resting, and the other children are out riding so allow me to escort you, dear lady. We do not often get the chance to talk on our own.'

I inclined my head but said nothing as he fell into step beside me, and we walked out of the front door and down the short flight of steps to the drive.

'You remind me of somebody.' Mark Cambridge strolled beside me, his shoulders slightly stooped, his hands clasped behind his back. 'From where do you come, Mrs. Moon? Is that really your name? it is quite delightful. And how did you become acquainted with my brother and his wife?'

'I would rather not talk about myself. My life is private and so long as Mr. and Mrs. Cambridge are satisfied with my services, I do not think that my personal history is any concern of yours.' I spoke quickly, lengthening my stride, praying that he would not remember.

Not little Tabitha Thomas who had run wild in the woods and fields as a child; not the gamekeeper's daughter, who had often seen the Cambridge boys out riding, both of whom had been taught to shoot by my father.

'It is the eyes,' he remarked at my side, 'such an unusual colour. But there — ' he checked himself — 'I'll not offend you further, Mrs. Moon. My sister-in-law is certainly most satisfied with you, she sings your praises all day long. And my brother — ' he paused, laughter in his voice — 'my brother is unusually reticent. As he is the last man to remain unaware of female charms, I think that he, too, is well satisfied.'

I stopped walking and turned to face him. 'It would be best if we went our separate ways, sir. Your talk offends me and I have no intention of continuing with this conversation.'

'Ah, Mrs. Moon, forgive me.' He placed a hand lightly on my arm and his voice was contrite. 'I will say no more on a subject which is distasteful to you. What I really wanted was to enlist your aid.'

I frowned and then continued walking. 'How can I possibly help you?'

'You can do much if you feel so inclined. Listen. There is to be a ball held here shortly, as you know, a sort of home-coming celebration for me.'

I nodded. We had all been discussing the forthcoming event and Sylvia and I had been spending long hours with Miss Trundle being fitted for our new gowns. Mine was to be made of ivory-coloured tulle, with pearls being used to gather in festoons the flounces of the skirt. I was to have a hair-net embroidered with pearls to hold back my thick brown hair, and a cordon of pearls to pass across my brow. Sylvia was lending me a fan, inlaid with mother-of-pearl, and I had new white satin slippers to go with the gown.

I was a little nervous, for both the Cambridge sisters would be coming, but as they were both married ladies now with children of their own, it seemed highly unlikely that they would remember me. At first I had intended staying upstairs, to keep Harriet company for the evening, but Sylvia had insisted that I attend the ball and Mr. Cambridge had not gainsaid her.

'Primrose would dearly love to join in the dancing, Mrs. Moon,' Mark Cambridge went on, 'she is having a gown made especially for the occasion, I believe, and I want her to be there. I am quite taken with my little niece,' he said smiling, 'and the feeling is mutual, as perhaps you have realized. I do beg you, dear madam, to have a word with my brother. He insists that Primrose is too young to attend and must watch the dancing from the gallery, with the other children. But she is a young lady, Mrs. Moon, and most mature in thought, and I wish to dance with her.'

'Do not lose your heart to her.' I looked up at his set face. 'She is very young still and I am sure that Mr. Cambridge has ambitious plans for his beloved daughter. Besides, you are too closely related.'

'Perhaps,' he shrugged, 'if Philip is indeed her father. But who knows if he is? His reputation was such that any girl could have foisted her illegitimate baby onto him, and he would have been the last to know if it were really his. What is praiseworthy, of course, is the fact that he accepted three such bastards and gave them his name.'

I was silent. I knew the truth and could confirm the relationship between Primrose and Mr. Cambridge; I had watched my mother die and seen the baby girl at its moment of birth. But my testimony must remain unspoken.

'I ask only that she attend the ball,' he went on. 'It would be most unfair to exclude her. Say that you will speak to Philip on our behalf, Mrs. Moon.'

'I shall do what I can.'

Primrose was mature in some ways; she had drooped around like a true love-sick maid ever since Mark Cambridge had come back. But he was far too old for her; perhaps Mr. Cambridge was right in forbidding her to come downstairs for the dancing.

'Why have you not married, sir? You must have had many a girl swooning over you in America?'

He smiled. 'The American ladies are a little too emancipated for me, Mrs. Moon. I prefer the old-fashioned girls over here. And maybe, like my brother in the past, I intend enjoying myself before becoming tied to a wife and family.' He sighed. 'But I am reaching an age when I feel it would be pleasant to settle down and become a country gentleman. I am looking for an estate of my own, and once somewhere suitable is found no doubt I'll wed.'

'But do not think about Primrose,' I said firmly. 'She is still in the schoolroom, so do not allow her appearance to blind you to that fact.'

'She is quite beautiful,' he agreed softly, 'I have never seen a girl as lovely as she is.'

'Maybe, but not for you.'

'That is for me to decide.' He laughed and his face lightened dramatically. 'We are being very serious, Mrs. Moon, and it is far too nice a day for sombre thoughts. Now, as you will not talk about yourself I shall tell you what life is like on the other side of the Atlantic.'

We spent the rest of that walk in pleasant conversation, for he was an eloquent speaker and had much to say about the country he had recently left.

On the night of the ball I was excited, but a little worried lest one of the Cambridge sisters recognize me. I knew that I looked my best and was anticipating an enjoyable few hours, for I loved dancing and had not heard music for a long time. But I dreaded seeing the Cambridge family en masse and did not like the idea of having to dance with Philip Cambridge.

When the Cambridge sisters arrived, accompanied by their husbands, Sylvia introduced me and they both nodded coolly without a flicker of recognition;

probably thinking that it was presumptuous of me to appear at such a gathering, for I was only a paid companion and had no right to be clad in such an expensive and beautiful gown.

The elder, Miss Gwendoline that was, had lost her former plumpness and was now a sharp-nosed, sharp-tonged matron, looking rather like her older brother. But Verona still had a childish air about her and looked red-faced and bewildered in a blue gown festooned with white satin bows. They were both frigidly polite to me but Sylvia championed me nobly, and I stayed close by her side except when one or other of us were dancing.

Mr. Cambridge danced once with his wife, once with each of his sisters, and with Primrose, then he advanced on me. As I tried to relax in his arms and enjoy the lovely lilting melody of the waltz, I looked across the crowded ballroom straight into the eyes of Mr. Anthony Warren. He was standing alone by the door, presumably having just entered, and he looked very surprised and very angry.

'What is it? Are you not feeling well?' Mr. Cambridge's hand tightened on my waist as I brought my stricken gaze back to his face, feeling the blood drain from my head.

'I feel faint,' I whispered, 'I must get out — have some air.'

He led me through the dancers to the glass doors which were open on to the terrace. 'My dear, Mrs. Moon, you look terrible. Sit here awhile.' He helped me to the stone bench which stood beneath one of the windows. 'I'll fetch some wine — do not move.' And he vanished back into the ballroom.

The soft night air revived me and the darkness calmed my racing heart. Wishing that I were not so tightly laced, I put a hand to my head. What was going to happen now? Could I escape upstairs without anyone seeing me? What excuse could be given for my departure? Dear heavens, what a predicament — he was the last man I had expected to see on the estate!

When I heard footsteps crunching beside me I looked up, expecting to see my employer returning, but there, in the light from the window, stood Mr. Warren.

His face was like the carved marble of a statue as he towered over me.

'What a surprise. Tell me — er — Mrs. Moon — what brought you to this part of the world? And where is your dear husband? I found out a little about you from Mrs. Cambridge, you see.' His voice was light, but I could hear the anger beneath his words.

'Please,' I strove desperately for control, 'please do not say that you know me. It is vital that my past be hidden from . . . '

'Here you are.' Mr. Cambridge returned, a glass in one hand, and I took it from him thankfully holding it to my lips for a long moment.

'Allow me to introduce you, Warren,' he said. 'This is my wife's friend and companion, Mrs. Moon, and this is an old school friend of mine, ma'am, Mr. Anthony Warren.'

Mr. Warren bowed over the hand which I extended to him and his fingers, as they touched mine, were as cold as his face.

'Mrs. Moon is suffering momentarily from the heat of the ballroom. Stay with her for a while, Warren, if you would. I must return to my guests.'

Then Mr. Cambridge left me alone with the last man I wanted to see, or be near.

'Well?' His voice sounded above me. 'I am waiting for an explanation.'

I cupped my hands around the glass, willing my lips not to tremble. 'I cannot explain now, it is such a long and complicated story. Only be so kind as to keep silent on your knowledge of me and my past, sir.'

'By God, Tabitha!' He exploded suddenly into wrath. 'That is not good enough. I rescued you from the gutter, fed and clothed you, gave you a first-class education, sent you to the continent and lavished on you all the luxuries and comforts within my power, and you showed your gratitude by running off without a word of explanation! For three years I have heard not one word from you and now find you ensconced in the bosom of the Cambridge family, living like a queen — I *demand* to know the reason!'

'I cannot tell you.' I lowered my head, wishing that somebody would appear, that Sylvia would call for me, that the ground would open and swallow me up.

'You females are all the same,' he said, through his teeth. 'You take everything you can without gratitude, then run off like a whore with the first man who takes your fancy. I should have left you in the gutter, Miss Thomas — there is no Mr. Moon, is there? The gutter is where you belong. I wonder how Cambridge would react if I told him some truths about you? How you accosted me — smelly and filthy

— as a 13-year-old urchin? How I took you in and gave you a home? How you rewarded me by stealing jewellery and running off in the middle of the night? Shall I tell him that, Tabitha Thomas?'

'Stop!' I cried. 'I'll hear no more.'

He ignored me. 'What are you after now, my dear? Mrs. Cambridge's husband, or her jewels?'

'It is not what you think — I have a reason, but not those that you are saying.' I sprang to my feet and made to push past him back into the ballroom. 'Please go away and leave me in peace.'

'Not so fast.' Mr. Warren swung round, catching hold of my arm and his fingers bit into my flesh making me cringe from the pain. 'You are a wanton and a thief, miss, but if Cambridge can enjoy your body, then, by Jove, so shall I!'

He pulled me roughly against him, his free hand going to my head, clasping the heavy fold of hair in its pearled net, pulling back my head so that my face was uplifted to his. Then his mouth was on mine, hard and cruel, hurting me with its passion.

I could not move, could scarcely breathe, and yet in that moment before I began to struggle, my heart leapt within my breast and for an instant my lips responded to his. This was different! This man could arouse my emotions as Philip Cambridge had never done. This was right, this was good; it was exciting and frightening and completely overwhelming.

Pulling my shattered nerves together and gathering my wits, I remembered my vow, my plans for revenge, and realized that if my employer should return and find me in the arms of Mr. Warren, all was lost.

Lifting one foot I kicked at Mr. Warren's shin as hard as I could. My slippers were soft and the blow was impeded by my petticoats, but he was surprised into relaxing his grip on me and I was suddenly free.

Putting a hand to my hair which was beginning to tumble down my back, I rescued my pearl net, then stood back and glared at my companion.

'I am not a thief,' I said fiercely. 'I sold my jewellery, yes, but it was *mine*, and as you kept me totally penniless there was no other way for me to get hold of some money. And this — this coming here was necessary, no, it was essential! I hate Philip Cambridge and would never be here with his family from choice. But I must remain for private reasons. I am not telling you what they are, and am no longer under your domination. Go back to London, Mr. Warren, and allow me to live as I please. I only pray that you will have the decency not to reveal my secret and thus upset everything that I have planned for years and years!'

I turned and ran from him, round the corner of the house, and he did not follow. There was a side door which was seldom used and I hoped that it would be open, allowing me to slip upstairs without seeing anyone and having to explain my dishevelled appearance.

Fortunately nobody was about and I gained the safety of my room and flung myself onto my bed in a torrent of weeping.

Suddenly, I did not hate Philip Cambridge enough to want to destroy him; my resolve melted with my tears and I wanted to creep away and hide from all the deceit and lying of the last years. I wanted to go back to London, to the safety and comfort of Mr. Warren's house; wanted to be spoilt and admired by him again, and yes, wanted to be loved by him. I had not realized that truth before.

Mr. Cambridge's love-making was abhorrent to me and I hated myself for allowing his embraces. I did not want to go ahead with my plan. My parents had died so long ago it would be better to forgive and forget. My courage had disappeared and with it had gone all desire for revenge.

I wanted Anthony Warren. The feeling of his arms about my body, of his lips on mine, was still warm within me, and I knew that I loved him, had probably loved him for a long time without being aware of it.

But it was too late. Lifting my wet face from the pillow, I pushed at my tangled hair. Too late for hope, too late for a decent life and the love of an honourable man. With a sickening feeling in my stomach I rose to my feet and walked over to the mirror. No good man would want me now that I had become Mr. Cambridge's mistress.

You will have to go through with it, Tabitha Thomas. I stared at my miserable countenance in the glass, at my tumbled hair, reddened eyes and bruised mouth. You have come this far and there is no turning back.

In the morning all was as it had been before. Mr. Warren had not spoken, Mr. Cambridge did not know the truth and I was bound to my vow as surely as the ivy is bound to the oak tree. But why had Mr. Warren not denounced me as he had intended? What had made him change his mind? I would never know, but for the moment was thankful for his reticence, for whatever reason it was which had made him hold his tongue on my behalf.

Sylvia had come to my room later that night, worried by my absence from the ball, and had accepted my excuse of a headache without question.

'Poor dear,' she had said soothingly, 'I know how abominable they can be. Go to bed, dearest, and do not worry about me. I shall get Fanny to assist me.'

To my relief Mr. Cambridge had not asked me to go to his room. He had been kept busy with his guests, and many of the gentlemen had not gone to bed at all but had stayed up smoking and drinking when the dancing ended. Mr. Warren had departed early for London, I learned, and had left without giving away my secret.

So I was safe, and must forget all about him and the emotions he aroused in me, and must remain and carry out the task for which I had come to Hertfordshire.

In the autumn of that year Mr. Cambridge began to sicken; nobody knew for sure what ailed him, and the local doctor fussed and fretted without, it seemed, having the least idea what to do. I played nurse, for Mr. Cambridge was short-tempered and impatient both with his own weakness and with everyone else's presence. Even Primrose was banned from his sight and I, alone, was expected to be always present, to hold his hand, wipe his brow and listen to his curses and muttering.

Sylvia was left entirely to Fanny's care, for I had no time for her and must be continually at her husband's beck and call. This did not bother me unduly, for it was a welcome change from his lovemaking and gave me a respite from Sylvia's continual chatter, but I was sad not to be able to see more of Harriet. I did manage to get up to her room every evening and give her a kiss and tell her a short story before she went to sleep. But there was no longer time to walk or play with her and she was more alone than ever, with both Primrose and Edward seeking Mark Cambridge's company at every opportunity. They went out riding at every spare minute, I gathered from Fanny, and Harriet was not fond of horses.

Oysters were blamed for Mr. Cambridge's malaise and this seemed a reasonable enough excuse, save for the fact that both Mark Cambridge and Sylvia had eaten of the same shellfish with no ill effects.

It was whilst Mr. Cambridge was still in bed, although seemingly on the mend, that one of the housemaids knocked timidly on the door of his bedchamber. I was reading aloud to my employer and let the book fall to my lap as I bade her enter.

'What now?' said Mr. Cambridge irritably. 'Can we never be left in peace?'

'Beg pardon, sir.' Molly dropped a curtsey, very red in the face. 'There's a young lad below, to see you, ma'am,' she glanced at me in a curious fashion, 'most insistent he is, and won't go away until you comes down to see him.'

'Who on earth can be wanting me?'

Was it some relation of Daisy's husband? But I had told her never to come up to the house. I used to visit her and William when I had an occasional free day.

'Mr. Knowles told me to come and fetch you, ma'am. He says he's your brother.'

'My brother!' I sprang to my feet, panic gripping my heart. 'But I have no brother.'

'What the deuce is going on?' Mr. Cambridge shifted on his bed. 'For God's sake go and see what is happening, Mrs. Moon, and then get back here at once, do you hear?'

'Yes, sir.' I followed Molly swiftly from the room. 'Did he give a name, Molly?'

'No, ma'am.' She tucked her chin in, her eyes sliding sideways to my face with the same peculiar look.

Downstairs in the big warm kitchen a thin and bedraggled figure stood before the range, steam rising from him in an ill-smelling cloud. Cook was busy at the scrubbed table, her head lowered, but the two little kitchen maids were agog in one corner, ostensibly peeling potatoes, but all their attention was on the lad and on me.

Molly stood to one side of the door, her finger pointing. 'That's him,' she announced.

I could feel colour flooding my cheeks as I moved forward.

'Who are you and what do you want with me?'

The youth turned at the sound of my voice and I saw that it was Tommy Marsh. Not much taller, shrunken in face and figure, but a young man, nonetheless, and little changed in feature.

'I've come to find you, Tabs. I've finished at the mill now and knew you'd be kind to me, like you was before.' His smile was brave but he looked starved and miserable and desperately pale.

Dear heavens, I thought, not more complications.

'How very foolish of you to say that you were my brother,' I remarked coldly, 'and I really don't know how I can help you. But come with me,' I went on quickly, aware of numerous pairs of listening ears, 'and we'll talk in the parlour. Molly,' I turned to the maid, 'tell the master that I won't be long and then please bring tea in to us at once.'

We went to the small sitting-room which Sylvia used in the mornings, but as she sat in the drawing-room in the afternoons we were unlikely to be interrupted here.

'How in heaven's name did you find me?' I stared at the scarecrow-like figure, furious at his intrusion into my life, not knowing how I was going to cope with this extra problem.

'I've finished me 'prenticeship, like I told you.' Tommy began to shiver and moved closer to the grate, where the remains of a fire flickered uncertainly. 'An' I couldn't stand being up north no longer so I comes down to London to look for you. 'Member what you told me, Tabs, that long ago at the Court? You said you was going to be a fine lady an' 'ave money, and all, and you've done it now, ain't you?' He looked at me with little Mary's eyes. 'You'll 'elp me, won't you, Tabs?'

'Sit down and dry yourself.' I moved to poke at the fire and then shovelled on some more coal. 'You'll get some hot tea in a moment. Dear God, did you have to choose such a day!'

The wind was lashing against the windows, making the panes rattle, and the rain had not ceased since early morning. Molly brought in a tray of tea and when she had gone I poured Tommy a cup and then sat in the chair opposite him and stared at his pathetic form.

'So you went to London?'

He nodded, gulping down the hot

liquid. 'To Paradise Court, but Ma ain't too well, and our Mary's gone and Meggie don't want me, so Ma said you should help.' He cupped his hands around his drink, his shoulders hunched. 'You owe our family something, don't you?'

'I owe your family nothing. But I'll not argue with you now. How did you find me *here*?'

'Ma said to follow the coachman what takes her money and 'e lives in a real grand 'ouse, and when we got talking 'e were good to me and said maybe you'd 'elp.'

So Mr. Warren still sent money to Mrs. Marsh? I was amazed. Particularly after the way in which I had behaved. But I would not think of him, nor of St. James's Square, or I should go mad with self-pity and regrets.

'Go on,' I said harsly, gripping my fingers together on my lap.

'An' the coachman, John 'e was, told me of this place in 'ertfordshire what 'e 'ad recently visited with 'is master, Mr. Warren. An' 'e said you was 'ere and known as a widow lady by the name of Mrs. Moon. So I comes, Tabs, 'cos you're the only person what 'as ever bin kind to me. And 'ere I am.'

'But what can I *do* with you?' I stood up and began to pace the room. 'I have my hands full as it is with a frail lady and her sick husband and three difficult children . . . ' I broke off; he was not interested in my problems. 'We don't need more servants in the house, Tommy, and you are far too weak to work on the estate. Heavens, what a predicament!'

'I ain't gonna work, Tabs, I'm gonna live proper, like you. I'll say I'm your brother and you can bring me up like a real gentleman and give me fine clothes and money and such like — Ma says so.' He gave a determined nod. 'You done it yourself so now you gotta 'elp me.'

I spun round on him, anger leaping in my breast. 'I'll do no such thing! And stop calling me Tabs. I've worked and schemed and striven for this all my life but I'll not see all my plans ruined by your miserable mother! I owe you nothing, Tommy Marsh, and paid my debt to your family years ago.'

He cringed from my wrath, his face crumpling. 'Then what am I to do?' he whined, his thin hands clasping his cup like a bird's claws. 'I don't know what'll 'appen to me — I ain't got no 'ome and Ma don't want me there in the Court. You gotta 'elp me.' He lifted his chin and there was a savage look in his eyes. 'I'll tell 'em all I knows about Paradise Court, and you living in all that rotten filth, and I'll say our Meg's a whore, and I'm your brother and they'll believe me, see if they don't!'

I could have shaken him.

'Shut your mouth, Tommy Marsh, and let me think!'

I bit my lip, frustration mingling with my anger, feeling helpless and afraid. He could undermine all that had been so carefully built up over the years; I could deny everything that he said, but it was obvious that we knew each other, and my past was decidedly vague. The Cambridges really knew very little about me. Oh, yes, they would believe him all right.

Yet, deep inside, I felt pity for the wretched lad, for his miserable existence at the mill, his poverty-stricken background and uncaring mother. I had clawed my way out of the mire; was there nothing I could do to help him now?

Then I thought of Daisy.

As we sipped our cups of tea, both grateful for the soothing beverage, I told Tommy about her and William and explained that for the moment he must go and live with them.

'You must give me time to think of a solution,' I said, 'and time to talk to my employer. For I am only a servant here, Tommy, albeit a rather superior one. I have wages paid to me, and could be dismissed tomorrow if I did not give satisfactory service. I am not the mistress of this house, and must ask permission for everything I do.'

This was not entirely true but my reasoning appeared to convince him.

'I can promise you a warm house and a comfortable bed with Daisy, and that I will help you all I can once we have come to a decision about your future. Just be patient, Tommy, and thankful for what can be arranged at this short notice.'

He nodded, looking very tired, and I realized that he had been under great strain, also.

'When did you leave London?' I asked.

'Yesterday afternoon,' he muttered, 'an' I slept overnight in a barn.'

I thought of 9-year-old Tabitha Thomas and her journey to London all those years ago, and how she had been rescued by Susan Marsh and given a place to live, and found somewhere to work. It was true, I owed this lad something, his family had given me support and succour when I had been most vulnerable.

So Tommy went to live with Daisy

and William, who took him in without questions and gave him a home whilst I grappled with my own problems. And they were manifold.

Sylvia was growing daily more difficult, as I spent extra time with her husband who lapsed again into sickness and did not leave his bed.

'I cannot live alone, Tabitha,' she wailed, 'if Mr Cambridge should die you must promise never to leave me. I cannot cope with those dreadful children and Primrose is so headstrong she will not obey me. Oh, dearie me, what shall I do?'

She wept often and long and Fanny would call me several times a day to say she did not know what to do with her mistress in these moods.

Primrose spent every possible minute in the company of Mark Cambridge, and they did not encourage Edward to join them now and would ride off for hours at a time, sometimes not returning until late in the evening. They would not listen to Sylvia and I did not have the authority to control them.

'What will people say?' moaned Sylvia. 'A young girl should not go riding about the countryside in the company of a man for hours on end. Her reputation will be ruined even if he is her uncle. And she will not do her lessons — Miss Graham is always coming and complaining to me. And *I* do not know what to do.'

Edward, too, was refusing to do his schoolwork and Miss Graham was left with gentle little Harriet, who tried to seek my company and for whom I no longer had time.

'Everything will be all right soon,' I told the child, kissing her good-night one evening, when I had managed to escape from Mr. Cambridge's room for a few precious minutes.

But Primrose and Edward made the most of their father's absence from the household and the servants became lazy and slapdash with a weak mistress and a master who was confined to his bed.

In the midst of all the turmoil I

prayed for the end to come; it was all a terrible strain and I was regretting my past actions. My aim had almost been achieved, but my hatred for Philip Cambridge had diminished once he was helpless and bed-bound, and I felt only pity for him now, wondering how long it would be before my own strength gave out and I became a snivelling, whining wretch like my mistress. For I was very tired, and oddly depressed, watching over the man night and day, sleeping seldom and constantly having to tend to his needs.

One evening, late in November, he indicated that he had something to say, so I pulled my chair closer to his bed and bent over him.

'I shall die soon, Mrs. Moon, and must admit it now.' His voice was a whisper but his words were clear. 'You are strong and courageous and I leave my wife and children in your care. Look after them.'

I nodded and he reached out and took hold of one of my cold hands.

'One thing more.' His voice thickened and he coughed and winced. 'I have never told a soul but now you must know. Primrose and Mark must not marry. Do you hear? On my death you must tell them the truth.' His voice faded and I bent nearer. What did he want to say? 'Primrose is not my daughter, Mrs. Moon.'

Ice-cold fear rippled down my spine as I stiffened, my nostrils arching with shock, my throat as dry as sand.

'What are you saying? What do you mean?' I croaked.

'Mark is her father, Mrs. Moon. You must tell them that. They must know at once, before it is too late.' His chest heaved with the effort to speak. 'You *must* tell them — now!'

He fell back upon his pillows, sweat shining upon his brow.

'How do you know this? Are you certain it is Mark?' I leaned forward urgently. 'Why did *you* claim her as your daughter? Oh, speak to me!'

Standing up I bent over him in

agitation, wiping his face with my handkerchief, willing him to say more. My heart was pounding within my breast and I felt dreadfully ill. It could not be true!

'Stop them, Mrs. Moon,' he whispered. Then his head fell sideways and his eyes closed.

I flung back the bedclothes and felt for his heart beat, it was there, a faint fluttering movement, no more. Leaping for the door I flung it open and raced along the passage to my room. Then I flung on my shawl and ran back to the stairs, screaming for Fanny, for Mr. Knowles, for anyone who could hear me.

Doors opened, footsteps echoed across the hall, voices were raised in alarm and confusion.

'Send for the doctor, quickly, and get the carriage for me. The master is dying and needs help urgently. I must get to London, at once, damn it! Hurry — all of you!'

There were minutes of commotion;

someone was sent on horseback for the doctor in the village, the horses and carriage were summoned for me and I waited, fretting, desperate to be off.

As I stood in the hall, chewing at my lip, Sylvia appeared at the top of the stairs.

'Have they been caught?' she called down, her face a white blur above me.

'What are you talking about?' I said impatiently.

'Why, Mark and Primrose,' she answered, beginning to descend the stair. 'I thought that was what all the fuss was about.' She giggled, a silly, breathless sound. 'They are naughty and I don't know *what* Mr. Cambridge is going to say when he finds out. Miss Graham brought me the letter just now, she found it in Primrose's room.'

I swayed, clutching at the marble-topped table at my side.

'What are you saying?' I whispered, my throat so tight that I could not speak aloud.

'Why, that they have run off to be

married, dearest. Primrose said she knew her father would not agree and as she and Mark love each other they have eloped. My goodness, you do look bad, dear. Won't you sit down?'

10

It was after midnight when I reached St. James's Square, and I hammered on the door willing Arnold to wake up quickly and let me in. Eventually the door was opened and the butler looked astounded as I pushed past him into the hall.

'Wake Mr. Warren immediately — this is a matter of extreme urgency. He must come down at once, at *once*, do you hear, man?'

Arnold drew himself up, indignation written all over his sombre countenance.

'Yes, miss. If you will wait in the library I shall call him directly.'

'Please hurry.'

He lit a candle from the one he held in his hand, then leaving me to enter the dark library alone, he made his way up the staircase into the shadows above.

I placed my candle upon the mantelshelf. The fire had died down and there were but a few smouldering embers in the grate. Rubbing my hands together, chilled to the bone by fear, I paced the room, longing for the sight and sound of Mr. Warren.

He appeared in a very short space of time, a maroon-coloured dressing-gown covering his tall frame, his hair ruffled.

'What in God's name is going on?' he asked angrily.

'You must help me!' I flew at him, clasping my hands before me, the words spilling out in wild confusion. 'Philip Cambridge is dying and it's all my fault and you must get a doctor — the best there is — someone of great knowledge and experience, who will save him. Oh, fetch someone now, sir, and go to Hertford, or Mr. Cambridge will die and I shall never forgive myself. And Primrose and Mark have eloped and he is her father and it is all too dreadful!'

I burst into a torrent of weeping, covering my face with my hands.

'You are demented, Tabitha,' my companion said coldly. 'Stop that noise at once and explain immediately what this is all about.'

'There is no time,' I shrieked, lifting my head and glaring at him through my tears. 'Don't you understand? Mr. Cambridge is dying and must have expert attention at *once*. I have sent for our local doctor but he is an ignorant old man, and those two must be stopped before they . . . '

'Why is Philip dying?' cut in Mr. Warren brusquely. 'He was perfectly fit the last time I saw him. Why, he is a man in his prime. You are exaggerating.'

'I am not! I have poisoned him — I did it on purpose — that was my plan all along, the reason why I went there in the first place, and why I could not tell you when you asked. But it was a terrible mistake — he is not to blame — and I cannot let him die, I cannot!'

'Dear heavens.' Mr. Warren put a hand to his head and ruffled his hair further. 'Either you are mad, or I am.

Do you mean to tell me that you have been poisoning your employer?'

I nodded, unable to speak. More than ever aware of my terrible, unnecessary crime.

'But why? No, I'll have explanations later.' Suddenly he sprang into action, moving to the door, shouting for Arnold, vigorous and powerful. Just as I had hoped he would be.

'What did you give him, damn you?' He flung back at me over his shoulder.

'Deadly nightshade berries — I squeezed them into his drink at night.' I quailed before his look of fury.

'Go up to your room and stay there until I get back,' he said through his teeth. 'Arnold, get me the carriage at once and then give orders for someone to wait on Miss Tabitha. She is not to leave this house until my return, and must be attended for every minute of the day and night. Hurry, man, I must be away at once.'

He departed and I heard his footsteps thudding up the stairs. Arnold also vanished and I sank down upon the chair by Mr. Warren's desk, my head bowed. Please God, I prayed desperately, let him be able to do something. Let him be in time.

⋆ ⋆ ⋆

For one week I remained closeted in the small bedroom on the top floor. I lay in bed for most of the time, refusing to get dressed, eating and drinking but little. Mrs. Caroline appeared the next day and she and a new maid, whom I did not know, shared the watch over me. I would not speak, would not answer Mrs. Caroline's tentative questions; waited only for the sound of Mr. Warren's voice, for the news that he would bring with him when he came.

I lay in misery, remembering all that had passed, wondering if Philip Cambridge could be saved, reliving every moment of my perfidy.

But how could I have known? He had kept secret the vital knowledge of

Primrose's parentage, how could I have known that he was not the girl's father? I tried to ease the guilt in my mind, it was not my fault that he had been punished. But of course it was.

I lay in a tight mound of self-pity, hugging my legs to my breast, knowing that death awaited me. For I had committed murder, or attempted it, and the law would have no mercy on a female who had acted in such a vile fashion. True, Mr. Cambridge had made me suffer, had caused me to feel both pain and degredation. I had loathed being his mistress and had wished to make him suffer, to hurt him as he had hurt me. But if this were all, I should not have contemplated killing him. One did not murder a person simply because one disliked him.

Philip Cambridge's death had been ordained because of his behaviour towards my mother — because he had caused both my parents to die. This had all been clear cut, simple logic. A child's vow had been fulfilled.

But if he had not seduced my mother, if Primrose was not his daughter and he had played no part in my parents' deaths, then I was lost indeed — without redemption. For I had murdered an innocent man and such action could never be forgiven.

One week later Mr. Warren returned.

The first I knew in my half-conscious state was the sound of movement below, a man's voice raised, breaking the awful silence of that house. Then Mrs. Caroline was on her feet opening the door to Mr. Warren, who fairly burst into the room.

'What's this? A sick-room? Dear God, I've had enough of them. What ails her, Mrs. Caroline? Why is she not up and dressed?'

'She has lain there this past week, sir, not speaking, scarcely moving. I really don't know what to do with her. Thank heavens you are back, sir, this is all quite beyond me.' The woman's voice was bewildered.

'Get up, Tabitha.' Mr. Warren loomed

beside me, as I turned my head to stare up into his ferocious countenance. 'Up at once, girl, then come down to the library. I want words with you.'

'I do not think she is able.' Mrs. Caroline hovered uncertainly beside him. 'She is very weak.'

'I want her dressed and downstairs within ten minutes, or I'll come up and drag her down myself.' He turned on his heel and left the room without waiting for a reply.

'Dearie me, Tabitha, I really do not know what is going on but you have angered him greatly. What did you do, child? And why did you run away like that, after all that he had done for you?' She chided and coaxed and helped me to sit up, but I felt very unsteady and could not bear to face Mr. Warren's wrath.

'I cannot,' I whispered, falling back against the pillows. 'Leave me alone. I want to die.'

He had not said one word about Philip Cambridge and his face had been like thunder. I could not face him. Mr. Cambridge was dead and it was all my fault and I did not want to go on living.

'You must try, dear, else he'll be true to his word and come up and drag you downstairs in your night attire. And what *will* the servants think?' Mrs. Caroline was trying to remove my night-gown, her face puckered with concern.

'They are gossiping enough as it is, but I cannot allow you to be hauled about like — like a cavewoman! And Mr. Warren has a vicious temper, he will do as he says, Tabitha, and you cannot be disgraced in such a manner. Come, dearie, I shall help you. Be a good girl, now, and I'll come with you. Dearie me, you're so weak you can scarcely walk.'

She had me dressed eventually and my hair was drawn back from my face with a ribbon and slippers were thrust upon my naked feet.

'There now, make an effort, dear, and

hold on to me. I'll not let you fall.'

Slowly, feeling faint and breathless, I allowed Mrs. Caroline to lead me down the stairs. We were just in time, for as we rounded the last landing and began the final descent, Mr. Warren shot out of the library and was about to mount the first flight.

'About time, too.' He stepped back as he saw us and waited as we moved slowly down towards him. 'In there.' He jerked his head at the library door.

Mrs. Caroline escorted me into the room and sat me down on the chair beside the fire.

'She is very frail — have you perhaps some brandy, sir?'

'She is as strong as a horse, and you may leave us, ma'am,' he barked. 'Do not return until I ring for you.'

She curtseyed, casting a frightened look at me, and then departed. Mr. Warren shut the door firmly behind her and then marched to the fireplace, where he took up a position frowning down at me.

'You deserve to be horse-whipped,' he said. 'How fortunate for you to be in such a feeble condition. I would have taken joy in administering the beating, myself.'

I lifted my head and gazed up at him. 'Mr. Cambridge?' I said, through parched lips.

'He'll live.' Mr. Warren returned my gaze, his dark eyes burning into mine. 'Luckily he has a strong constitution, and you can thank God on your bended knees, miss, that I was able to take an eminent physician down to Hertfordshire with me, and that his knowledge was such that he was able to save Cambridge. Otherwise, you would soon be feeling the touch of a rope around that slim neck of yours, and your dainty feet would be dangling some distance from the ground.'

'Don't!' I covered my ears with my hands, nausea rising within me.

'No, it is not pleasant to die. Perhaps you should have thought about that before carrying out your fiendish scheme.'

He turned and pulled a chair towards him, then sat down upon it stretching out his long legs towards the fire.

'Now, young lady, I want a full explanation of everything you have done since leaving this house three years ago.'

I put a hand to my head. 'I am too tired and cannot think straight — you must give me more time.'

I felt sick and very weary, but the relief was enormous. Philip Cambridge lived!

'You may take as much time as you wish, Miss Thomas, but you'll not leave this room until I have finished with you. And that will be when I know the whole story.'

Mr. Warren shifted into a more comfortable position and waited.

I sat with my head bowed. It had all begun with the death of my parents, but that seemed so very long ago now it scarcely mattered any more.

'Well?' My companion's voice broke in to my thoughts.

'I was born and brought up on the Cambridge estate,' I said slowly, lifting my head and returning his gaze. 'My childhood was very happy and I adored my mother.' I hesitated. 'She was quite beautiful, in fact Primrose looks very like her.' The thought of Primrose brought me back to the present with a jerk. 'Did you find them — her and Mark? Have they been stopped and told the truth?'

Mr. Warren nodded. 'We managed to track them down before they were wed and both are now home again. Go on, Tabitha, I want the rest of your tale.'

'My father was gamekeeper for the Cambridge family, and although I knew all the children by sight, they scarcely knew that I existed. I was but a working-class brat, after all.' My lip curled as I remembered Philip Cambridge's scornful words. 'But I was happy, until something went wrong

271

with my safe little world. Mother became silent and depressed, quite unlike her normal lively self, and I realised that she was to have another child. I did not know it then, but the doctor had warned her not to have any more children after me, and this baby was not my father's.'

I swallowed back tears of weakness, clasping my hands tightly together on my lap. 'Father told me all this on the night she died, when we sat together watching over her. And her last words to me were Philip Cambridge's name.' I stared across at my companion. 'She spoke his name with her dying breath,' I repeated fiercely, 'and with his reputation of course I believed him to be the father. Why did she say it? What did she mean?'

'Cambridge told me that he had felt pity for your mother when she went to him in her distress. His own father had died by then, and as he was head of the family, he decided to bear full responsibility. Mark was only 17 at that time and still at school, knowing nothing of the havoc he had caused. The young fool! Presumably your mother was trying to tell you to go to Cambridge and he would care for the babe.'

I nodded. 'Perhaps. They were no good, that family, both boys were spoilt and strong-willed and did whatever they pleased. Then Father killed himself, he could not bear to live without Mother, and all happiness ended for me. My dislike of the Cambridge family turned to hatred and I made a vow to get revenge, Mr. Warren, and I almost succeeded.'

Bitterness returned, and anger, and I was strengthened by my emotions. So arrogant and careless — both of them! But why had my mother succumbed to a mere schoolboy? It was hard to understand.

I took my mind back to memories of Father, and to the young, fair-haired Mark Cambridge, him who had kissed me with berry-stained lips. The younger brother had been full of laughter and energy, even then. He was also charming and carefree and had not offended me with his chatter and light-hearted flirtation. How much more attractive would he have seemed to a woman, still young and very lovely? And it had often struck me that Mother seemed to be years younger than my father. Doubtles the handsome young Cambridge boy had proved irresistible, particularly as Father had never been a jovial sort of man. But he had loved her.

Shivering, I held my arms tightly around my body. What a tragic ending to a summer's-day romance; so many lives affected by a few stolen kisses.

'Why was it *my* family which had to suffer?' I said. 'Why should not the Cambridges also bear some sorrow for their past actions?'

'But you saw to that, did you not, Tabitha? Philip Cambridge almost died. Are you not satisfied?'

'I would not want him dead, not now,' I answered wearily. 'I am drained of all hatred. These past weeks have not been pleasant.'

'That I can believe.' Mr. Warren rose and rang the bell. 'We will partake of some refreshment and you may finish your tale, meanwhile. How did Primrose come to enter that household?'

'I took her there, dumping her into the butler's arms early one morning and then running away as fast as I could.' I smiled despite my weariness. 'Bates looked very surprised. But he must have become used to it — I believe both Edward and Harriet were abandoned on the doorstep of the manor in later years.'

'You must have started the fashion,' remarked my companion drily. 'At least Cambridge took them in and accepted them. Many men would not have been so good-hearted.'

'Men are cruel beasts,' I replied bitterly. 'It is always the females who have to suffer.'

'Not always.' Mr. Warren gazed into the fire. 'Now that you have bared your soul, I shall admit my past to you. This is a night for reminiscence, it seems.'

At that moment Arnold knocked and entered, bearing a tray of food. To my surprise I was famished and bit into the piece of pie which Mr. Warren passed to me, with astounding appetite. He also poured me a glass of brandy, and the golden liquid warmed and relaxed me.

'It is not always the women who suffer,' Mr. Warren repeated when we were alone again. 'My mother cheated on my father and broke both our hearts when I was 14. I saw her in the stables, Tabitha, caught her with one of the grooms, and that memory has never left me.' His face was grim and he left the food untouched beside him. 'I, too, made a vow. That is why I can understand how you felt. I vowed that no female would ever touch my heart so long as I lived.'

'I'm sorry,' I whispered. 'I did not know that, although Daisy once told me that my room upstairs had been occupied by your mother.'

Mr. Warren nodded, reaching for his glass and drinking deeply. 'Father allowed her to stay here, but it was imprisonment. She never left that room except to come downstairs and play hostess on the few occasions when he desired her presence. Father had to keep up appearances, of course, and was too proud to let the world know that he had married a slut.'

'What happened to them both?'

'My father died some years ago and I, Tabitha, was neither so forgiving nor so merciful. I had her put into an asylum and she remains there still.'

I stared at him in horror. 'But she was not insane?'

'No, but she had to be punished. Like you, my dear, I desired revenge.'

'You are a hard man, sir. For I, at least, have repented of my sins and am thankful for a happy ending to my story. Was Mr. Cambridge — ' I hesitated — 'was he very angry?'

'Angry? More astonished, I think, that a mere female should have acted with such calculated ferocity. 'Tis a pity he has a wife — I believe he rather admires you.'

'After what I did to him?' I felt my face burn and lowered my head away from my companion's searching gaze. 'I must not condemn you, sir, when I acted in such a callous and wicked fashion. May God forgive me.'

To think that I had lain in Philip Cambridge's arms, allowed him to kiss and caress me, whilst all the time planning his murder! Dear heavens — what was to become of me?

'Do they all know?' I asked dully. 'Does Sylvia know what I did? Have the children been told?'

'Good Lord, no.' Mr. Warren spoke impatiently. 'It was my duty to tell Mr. Groves, the physician, so that he would know how best to handle his patient. Cambridge, I told, because I wanted to know why you had acted in such an abominable manner towards him. Once he was on the mend we discussed you and your past, and he remembered your parents, and of course it became clear to us then that you were out for revenge, believing that Philip was Primrose's father. Rest assured, Tabitha, Mrs. Cambridge and the family believe only that you rushed to London in order to summon a more qualified doctor to help.'

'Thank you for your discretion,' I said.

At least I would be able to hold my head up without shame if ever I saw Sylvia again.

'Now,' said Mr. Warren, straightening in his chair and glancing at the clock upon the mantelshelf, 'it is time you went to bed. I shall see you in the morning and we will doubtless both feel better after a night's sleep.'

* * *

The next morning, after having partaken of breakfast in my room, Mr. Warren asked to see me in the drawing-room. I felt stronger and in much better spirits than the day before and wondered what he had to say. He indicated the sofa with a nod of his head and I sank down upon it and waited.

'I have decided, Tabitha, that you and I will wed,' he announced abruptly.

I stared at him in astonishment. 'But you said that you would never marry, and I have acted most viciously, no one could ever trust me now!'

He smiled somewhat grimly. 'The world will be a safer place if you are in my care, Tabitha. You obviously need looking after and I believe myself to be the right man to have charge of you.'

'So that you can put me away when I annoy you? No, thank you, sir.'

I had thought myself to be in love with him once, would have liked nothing better than to have been his bride — once. But too much had happened since; I knew more about him now and the thought of his poor mother locked away like a lunatic for careless behaviour in her youth was intolerable.

'I would never put myself in your care,' I said firmly.

'Then why are you here, Tabitha Thomas? Why did you come to me for aid?'

'Because I knew no where else to turn, because you were an old friend of the Cambridges and were also a man of experience and knowledge. I *had* to have help, urgently, and you were the right person then.' I shrank back on the sofa. 'But you have no heart, sir, and I could not live with a man who did not know how to love.'

'Perhaps I could learn.' His eyes appeared very dark in his pale face as he stared back at me. 'Perhaps I could learn compassion, also. You have experienced much in your short life, and there is a lad in Hertfordshire who was enquiring most eagerly about your welfare. Tommy Marsh, by name. He said you were the only person who ever showed him kindness.'

'Tommy!' I put my hand to my head. 'I had forgotten about him. Is he all right? Is he still with Daisy?'

Mr. Warren nodded. 'And she is another who was cared for by you. Marry me, Tabitha, and we will share our life and perhaps help others less fortunate than ourselves.'

'Mrs. Marsh,' I muttered, 'you still send money to her. So you are not so heartless as you seem. Why did you continue to care for her after I ran away from you?'

He smiled. 'I told you that I once made a vow and it remained good until I met a ragged little chit, who offered her services to me late one night in the Haymarket. I took the creature in, Tabitha, and had a terrible time trying to make it more civilized. And whilst I was battling to educate this — this urchin, it stole my heart and I have not been the same man since.'

He moved from where he was standing and came to lean over me. Then, taking my hands in his, he pulled me to my feet.

'You made me suffer intolerably,

returning from the continent far more beautiful than any female deserves to be. I fell in love with you, Tabitha, much against my will, and when you ran away I was devastated.'

Mr. Warren lifted his hands from mine and gripped my shoulders, giving me a none too gentle shake.

'And so, my dear, now that I have you with me once more, I am not letting you go again whether you like it, or not.'

He lowered his head and his mouth closed on mine, hard and determined.

'I am going to kiss you and love you every day and night until you consent to be my wife,' he said against my lips.

I tried to pull away but his hands held me firm against him.

'Say yes.'

'I cannot . . . '

'Say yes, damn you!' His lips bruised mine until I was quite breathless.

'I cannot speak!' I managed to free myself from his grasp. 'How can I answer when you use me thus?' I looked up into his face and saw such love in his eyes, mingled with laughter, that my heart betrayed me. I did love him, most dearly, and would always love him. I knew that now.

Laying my head against his shoulder, I felt his arms tighten around me and a feeling of great peace and contentment fell upon me.

'I do not know how you can want to marry me,' I murmured, 'after the way in which I have so foolishly behaved. How can you trust me again?'

'I shall trust you, Tabitha, and love you and take care of you always. It seems to me as if you need some tenderness, my strong, proud love.' His lips brushed my forehead. 'To think that I imagined you to be Cambridge's mistress — I was so racked with jealousy, yet all the while you were plotting his death!' Mr. Warren threw back his head and laughed aloud. Then he bent and lifted my chin with his finger. 'You are brave and stalwart and beautiful, my Tabitha,' he whispered, 'and I adore you.'

Before he could kiss me again I pulled back in his arms, my heart beginning to pound. Had he not realized? Did he not know the truth? Did he believe me to be totally innocent still?

'There is one thing,' I said slowly, wondering how best to say it, hoping that he *did* guess and that I was mistaken. 'In order to gain Mr. Cambridge's confidence I had to get close to him — to — to win his affection.' I paused.

'I realise that Philip admired you, I told you that, dearest. Indeed, who could know you and not love you? That was why I behaved so badly at the ball — I was filled with envy, believing you to be his mistress. Forgive me, my love, for the cruel words I said.'

He bent to kiss me but I stepped back, my hands going to my breast.

'But I *was* his mistress!' A sob caught in my throat and my heart fluttered in anguish at the terrible look on his face.

'Oh, did you not realize that? But I did not love him. I hated him! All the time I hated him. But I had to do it, can't you see? There was no other way for me to get close to him — I *had* to gain his affection!'

'I do see, very clearly now.' Mr. Warren's voice was cold and his eyes were dead, empty of all love and laughter.

'Say you forgive me, or at least that you understand.' I pressed my hands to my trembling heart. 'I have never loved any man but you. That — all that I did with Mr. Cambridge was horrible and unreal. It was another reason I wanted him dead — I could not bear it any longer!'

'But you went to Hertfordshire in order to seduce him? You admitted that yourself. You chose to be his mistress? He did not force you?'

'No.' I lowered my head.

Useless to explain, to try and excuse my actions. I *had* gone to the manor with a set purpose, had meant Philip

Cambridge to take me to his bed, and, to be truthful, I had enjoyed having his money spent on me. I was a whore. There was no escaping from that fact.

Mr. Warren could never love me now and marriage was unthinkable.

I lifted my head and gazed at him for a long moment; at his dark hair and strong nose, at his wide mouth, unsmiling now and clamped shut, cruelly tight. I looked at his tall, wide-shouldered figure and at his beautiful, long-fingered hands. They would never hold me again, or touch my face, or caress me.

Remember these, I said to myself, remember these good things in your life. Then I turned and walked from the room and he did not try to stop me.

I went up to my room and collected my shawl. Everything else I left behind for nothing belonged to me, it was all Mr. Warren's. He had called me a thief once, a thief and a whore. The last I assuredly was, but I had no intention of proving him right about the first.

Downstairs I went, through the silent house, seeing nobody, and let myself out into the square.

All that day I walked the streets, wondering what to do, where to go. I could not return to Hertfordshire, memories were too painful and besides, I never wanted to see Philip Cambridge again.

It would be possible, I supposed wearily, to go back to Paradise Court, to share that horrible squalid room with Mrs. Marsh. But the thought of her malicious tongue and scornful eyes repulsed me. No doubt work could be found as a seamstress again, but three shillings and sixpence did not seem much to me now that I had grown accustomed to gowns of silk and taffeta and three meals a day and a warm bed. I would find it well-nigh impossible to live in poverty and could not imagine an existence on a few shillings a week.

There appeared to be only one thing at which I excelled. With my face and figure, I would have to follow Meg

Marsh's example and if it proved a slow and tortuous downhill struggle, so be it. I deserved punishment and would accept what Fate had in store for me.

Putting all thoughts of Anthony Warren to the back of my mind, with a stony heart and set chin, I made my way towards the Haymarket as a clock somewhere began striking the hour of ten.

For a moment I was taken back in time, hearing that same hour strike as, small and bewildered, I had arrived in the Strand, ready to make my fortune. But there was no Susan Marsh to rescue me this time and I was no longer a child, no longer innocent.

I pulled my shawl closer around my cold body and took shelter in a doorway as the crowds shouted and laughed and passed on by me.

A gentleman paused, staring at me in the darkness of the doorway, but as I straightened, about to force a smile to my lips, he went on with a curious shake of his head. Surprised, I turned away anxious to attract the attention of somebody else. I was hungry and becoming very cold and somehow must find a place for the night and, moreover, somebody who would pay me. I had no money and no jewellery to sell.

'Miss Thomas?' A man's voice spoke hesitantly behind me and as I swung round in astonishment I saw that it was the same young man who had recently passed me by. 'Is it Miss Thomas?' He peered intently into my face. 'Dear Lord, what are you doing here? I could not *believe* it was you!'

I looked up into the frowning, boyish countenance of Mr. Steven Arnott.

★   ★   ★

He took me home with him, back to his apartment in Jermyn Street, where his man brought us bowls of hot soup and pieces of pie. I was near to exhaustion by then and could scarcely speak, my teeth were chattering so wildly. But, in front of the warm fire, with food in my stomach and a friendly face on the other side of the hearth, I finally gave way to tears of relief and utter weariness.

'There, there,' said Mr. Arnott soothingly, thrusting a snowy white handkerchief at me and bending forward to hide his embarrassment by stoking up the fire.

I sobbed for several minutes, allowing the tears to wash away my guilt, to cleanse my very soul.

'What is going to happen to me?' I said at last, giving my nose a good blow and beginning to feel somewhat better. 'I seem to have done everything wrong and hurt a great many people, and now find myself in a worse state than ever before. What shall I do, Mr. Arnott?'

'You'd better start by telling me all about it,' he said matter-of-factly, looking more cheerful once I had stopped weeping. 'The last time I heard anything of you, you had vanished from Mr. Warren's house and he was distraught. What made you run away like that, Miss Tabitha? I wondered if you had eloped.'

I sighed and leaned back in my chair, closing my eyes. Then I told him exactly what I had done and he did not interrupt once. He just sat and listened as I talked and talked.

When I had finished my sad and sordid tale he blew out his cheeks and said, 'Phew!' and I thought how very young he looked; young and wholesome and kind.

'I do not suppose you would reconsider my offer of marriage?' he said earnestly, going red in the face. 'I should not mind about your past and I have a great admiration for you, Miss Tabitha.'

'Thank you.' I smiled across at him. 'You are the kindest man I have ever met and I hope that we shall always be friends. But you see, after all that I have been through, marriage to a man whom I did not love would be unthinkable.'

'And you love Mr. Warren?'

'Yes. He is the only man I shall ever love and of course he cannot marry me. His pride would never permit it and I, I am not worthy of him.'

'If he really loved you nothing would stop him making you his wife,' declared my companion stoutly. 'Loving is understanding another's misfortunes, and caring about them, and forgiving.'

'I wish there were more men like you,' I answered gently. 'Unfortunately, there is one law for gentlemen and another for their womenfolk. It is quite in order for a man to have a mistress and still remain an upright and honourable husband and father. But if a *female* should err from the path of righteousness — oh, dearie me, she is an outcast, and no respectable person will have anything to do with her.' I laughed, without humour. 'We must be perfect at all times, and put upon a pedestal and worshipped. We are not capable of vice, or carnal feelings, or dishonourable actions. We are *ladies*. I mean, they are. I am no longer one of

293

that breed and must learn to think and act as the being I have become — a fallen woman.'

'Indeed you are not!' My companion spoke with vigour. 'And I intend doing something about it. But first you must rest, Miss Tabitha, you look quite exhausted. Parkins has made my bed up for you with fresh linen, so go to my room now and have a good night's sleep. I shall see you in the morning.'

'But you,' I said, 'where will you sleep?'

'I shall be quite comfortable in here on the sofa. Good-night, Miss Tabitha, and forget all about today. Tomorrow we will make plans for your future.'

Epilogue

My husband had not wanted to attend the wedding.

'It will be an embarrassment to everyone,' he said. 'We are better here at home leaving the Cambridge family to their festivities on their own.'

'But I shall have to face them all one day,' I replied, 'and cannot hide away forever. This is surely a splendid opportunity to forget the past and look to the future. Besides, I promised Steven that I would go and he is my friend. I cannot let him down.'

'He is a friend indeed,' answered my husband soberly. 'If he had not come to me and been so persuasive, I should never have seen you again.'

He looked across at me and smiled. We were sitting together in the lovely Tudor drawing-room of our new home, with its black beams and ingle-nook fireplace, and my heart leapt within my breast as it always did when he was near. I loved him so much. Mr. Anthony Warren, who had finally forgiven me and made me his wife.

It had taken Steven Arnott several weeks to contact him, for after my last departure from St. James's Square, Mr. Warren had taken himself off to Paris, and the house had been shuttered and deserted save for the servants. But Steven had not given up hope and had called again and again until finally Mr. Warren returned from the continent and consented to see him.

I shall never know what words passed between the two men, but one morning when I was alone, there was a knock on the door of the Jermyn Street apartment and Mr. Arnott's man announced a visitor.

It was Anthony Warren.

I sat rigid in my chair, scarcely breathing, thinking that he had found out that I was staying with Steven Arnott and had come to accuse me all over again of immoral behaviour. It was true that I had lived in Steven's rooms during all those weeks, but it had been an innocent relationship and we had lived as happily and contentedly together as brother and sister. I did not deserve such kindness, but was intensely grateful as I had nowhere else to go, and allowed the days and weeks to slip by without thinking, or caring, about the future.

'I have come,' said Mr. Warren, standing just inside the door, his face gaunt, his eyes burning in his white face, 'because I cannot live without you, Tabitha. I have sought affection elsewhere, I have travelled abroad and striven to forget you. But every night your face has been before my closed eyes, and every day I have looked for you amongst the crowds. My life has been a torment of longing and loneliness and I cannot stand it any longer. Will you forgive me for my behaviour last time we met, and will you marry me?'

'Yes,' I whispered, unable to say more, looking at his beloved face through a sheen of tears.

He crossed the room in a bound, took me up in his arms and kissed me with a gentleness I had never known before.

We were married very quietly, with only Steven Arnott and one of Mr. Warren's oldest friends as our guests. Then we moved to this lovely old house in the Surrey countryside, which my husband bought for our marriage. London no longer held any charms for him and I revelled in the green fields and open spaces which I had loved so much in childhood.

Once we were duly established in our new home I asked that he would bring his mother to live with us.

'I want to help other people now,' I told him, 'I want to do good and make up for all the wretchednes of my past. Can you find it in your heart to forgive her and allow her to spend her last years in peace and comfort with us?'

Of course he agreed. My husband finds it difficult to refuse me anything and I, in a fever of charity, cannot do enough for those less fortunate than myself.

Mrs. Warren came to us, a frail, bewildered lady, who had once been beautiful. Her hair was snow-white and her troubled eyes were grey, with dark smudges beneath them. She seldom spoke and was startled easily at any sound or unexpected movement. She did not show surprise, or delight, at coming to live with us and I realized that we should not expect too much from her. Mrs. Warren dwelt in a world of her own and it did not seem likely that we would ever be able to reach out and draw her into our lives.

I did not reproach my husband; I had sinned enough myself and it was obvious that he was both perturbed and ashamed about his mother's mental condition. She was given two rooms on the ground floor for her personal use and I tried to encourage her to take meals with us and join us in the drawing-room in the evenings. But Mrs. Warren refused to leave her rooms and was looked after by one of the maids.

Soon after she joined us, it was arranged for Daisy and William to come down to our small estate. They had not been faring well in Hertfordshire and welcomed the chance to begin a new life with us. Daisy is becoming a most efficient and thrifty housekeeper and her William is helping on the estate. Tommy Marsh came too and is proving a reliable and honest servant.

It was when they were all assembled with us, and I had been brought up to date with their news, that I remembered little Harriet. I wanted her, too.

'She was not loved by Sylvia Cambridge, and her father had little time for her, preferring his older children. Can we not invite her for a visit, at least, and then see how we get on together?' I begged.

'Very well, if you insist.' But Anthony was not entirely happy with the idea.

'The child may come and stay, if that will satisfy you, but how do you intend getting her here? I will not travel to Hertfordshire to collect her,' he said grimly. 'I never wish to see Philip Cambridge again.'

Hope began to dwindle in my breast, it was inconceivable that I travel to fetch her, yet she was very young and could not undertake such a journey on her own.

Eventually, Steven Arnott came to the rescue. He was often down staying with us and both my husband and I looked upon him as one of the family.

'I shall go,' he said eagerly. 'It will be the simplest thing to help you out of your predicament. I shall be courteous to Mrs. Cambridge, for she was your friend, was she not, Tabitha? But I shall be coolly distant towards Mr. Cambridge and whisk the child away to you here where I know she will be content.'

He was so desirous of pleasing us that Anthony reluctantly agreed and Steven ventured forth, returning with my darling Harriet.

It was after her arrival that the miracle occurred, for Mrs. Warren took to her at once and in no time they were chatting together, and going for walks, and eventually joining us for meals. Harriet had never known a grandparent, and the gentle old lady filled a gap in the child's hungry heart. What stirred Mrs. Warren from her solitude I shall never know, but the little unloved girl and the misused older woman became firm friends and we were a united family at last.

I had written to Sylvia telling her of my marriage and we corresponded frequently after Harriet came to stay, although I had a strong suspicion that my former mistress would soon be inviting herself for a visit and I did not wish to see her. But Fate took a hand in our affairs, and Steven Arnott, dear kind boy that he is, fell in love with Primrose Cambridge the first time he set eyes on her.

I had heard from Sylvia that she was

a changed girl since learning the truth about her father. She had become silent and morose after Mark Cambridge's return to America, but Sylvia wrote that she was nevertheless polite and respectful at all times. A changed girl, indeed!

Steven, quite naturally, lost his heart to the beautiful unhappy girl and sought to amuse and cheer her. By the end of that summer he informed us joyfully that he had proposed marriage and been accepted.

It was a splendid match for her. Steven Arnott was an extremely wealthy young man, as well as being a very nice person, and I hoped that Mother, wherever she might be, could know of both her daughters' successful marriages.

'We must go to the wedding,' I said to my husband. 'Steven has entreated us to be present, and if I can bear the sight of Philip Cambridge, so must you.'

'I'd like to wring his neck,' muttered Anthony, 'damned scoundrel!'

'Now, now,' I said gently, laying a hand upon his arm, 'do not forget that it was I who was responsible for his actions, I who led him on and . . .'

'But that's just it!' My husband's temper flared and I shrank back in dismay, for he was normally the most even-tempered man and never angry with me. 'I *wish* to forget all about the past and your connection with that family. But seeing him again, and watching him look at you, knowing what he must be thinking, what he must be regretting . . .' He lowered his head, his fists clenching at his sides. 'It will be sheer Hell!'

'I'm sorry,' I whispered, 'I did not think. Then we will not go to the wedding. I shall write to Sylvia tonight and decline the invitation.'

But we went in the end. The Cambridge family had to be faced, as Anthony well knew, and this occasion would be the best way to meet. With Steven Arnott marrying my half-sister, we could not be forever making excuses and avoiding each other.

The marriage took place in the tiny church at Oakhurst and Primrose made a beautiful bride, appearing on her father's arm — I could not think of him as her uncle — in the same place that I had first seen her four long years before.

She wore a simple gown of white silk, trimmed with lace, with rosebuds in her hair and tucked into her bosom. She was very subdued and I prayed that Steven would not be disappointed in his wife. But he possessed love enough for two and his face fairly radiated adoration and pride.

Edward was there, a little remote, not quite knowing how to greet me, but Sylvia was overjoyed and embraced me warmly, patting and stroking my body as if she would never let me go. She asked when she could come for a visit and I said that we were making a great many changes to our home, but that she would be welcome once everything was in order. I knew that she would have to come eventually, but this gave me time in which to accustom myself to the idea.

Mr. Cambridge behaved impeccably, touching my cheek with dry lips, murmuring how pleasant it was to see me again, then removing himself to the other end of the room. I could see my dearest Anthony visibly relaxing as my old employer walked away.

Then it was my turn. Lifting my head and curving my reluctant lips into a smile, I took my husband's arm and led him forward.

'Come,' I said.

We approached the bridal pair and Anthony shook Steven Arnott by the hand and congratulated him.

I looked at Primrose and she gazed at me, dark hair springing from beneath the flowers on her head, eyes very blue in her pale face. Grief and shock had added maturity to her countenance since we had last met and she looked more like Mother than ever.

'God bless you,' I said softly, and my

smile came naturally and was not forced. 'I wish you all the happiness in the world.' And, leaning forward, I kissed my sister for the very first time.

THE END

We do hope that you have enjoyed reading this large print book.

Did you know that all of our titles are available for purchase?

We publish a wide range of high quality large print books including:
Romances, Mysteries, Classics
General Fiction
Non Fiction and Westerns

Special interest titles available in large print are:
The Little Oxford Dictionary
Music Book, Song Book
Hymn Book, Service Book

Also available from us courtesy of Oxford University Press:
Young Readers' Dictionary
(large print edition)
Young Readers' Thesaurus
(large print edition)

For further information or a free brochure, please contact us at:
Ulverscroft Large Print Books Ltd.,
The Green, Bradgate Road, Anstey,
Leicester, LE7 7FU, England.
Tel: (00 44) **0116 236 4325**
Fax: (00 44) **0116 234 0205**

A FRAGILE SANCTUARY

Roberta Grieve

When Jess Fenton refuses to have her disabled sister locked away, her employer turns them out of their cottage. Wandering the country lanes in search of work, they find unlikely sanctuary at a privately run home for the mentally ill — the very place that Jess had vowed her sister would never enter. As she settles into her new job, Jess finds herself falling in love with the owner of Chalfont Hall, even as she questions his motivation in running such a place.

SHIFTING SANDS

Shelagh Fenton

Ruth's father tells her that he has taken on Paul as a business partner, and whilst being obliged to co-operate with him, Ruth's reaction is to feel a deep distrust for a man she hardly knows. However, she comes to trust him and love him as they work together to track down her cousin Melanie, who has disappeared. Then Paul saves Ruth's life at serious cost to himself . . . just as they finally locate Melanie who is in great danger . . .

ONCE UPON A TIME

Zelma Falkiner

City girl Meredith plans to write a novel in the peace and quiet of the country, but finds her chosen retreat is over-run by a film production company. Despite her best intentions, she is soon lured from her story-telling into a make-believe world of early Australia, with handsome, bearded bush-rangers on horseback, and women in long skirts, boots and gingham bonnets. But in the real world, a little girl is in danger . . .